HOWLING AT THE HARVEST MOON

A SUSPENSE/THRILLER

ASH NIGHTENGALE

This is a work of fiction. Names, characters, places, and incidents are products of the author's imagination or are used fictitiously and are not to be construed as real. Any resemblance to actual events, locations, organizations, or persons, living or dead, is entirely coincidental.

World Castle Publishing, LLC
Pensacola, Florida
Copyright © Ash Nightengale 2021
Hardback ISBN: 9798499953709
Paperback ISBN: 9781956788051
eBook ISBN: 9781956788068
First Edition World Castle Publishing, LLC, November 1, 2021
http://www.worldcastlepublishing.com
Licensing Notes
Cover: Max Bray
Editor: Maxine Bringenberg

CHAPTER ONE

Gunner could see the white wisps of his breath as he methodically trekked his way through the dark forest. His only light was cast by a half moon that crept its way through a silhouette of outstretched limbs. He could see just fine after waiting for his eyes to adjust to the darkness, but a flashlight sat tucked away in his front pocket nonetheless. Gunner was trying to keep a steady pace without causing too much of a stir. He made sure to avoid fallen branches and bigger piles of noisy leaves as he tentatively meandered toward his destination. He brought his wrist up to his face and looked at the greenish glow. The watch said 3:54.

The diligent young man had made sure to park the SUV a good two miles off the main highway before strapping his rifle over his left shoulder and heading out on foot. He didn't want anybody to know where he was or what he was up to, at least for this particular hunt. In fact, he didn't even bother telling his wife. His night began by sneaking out of the house a little before 3:00 A.M.; that special time when even the drunks were getting home and crawling into bed, or at least passing out.

Gunner didn't mind rising so early. He liked the solitary moments and found a sense of tranquility,

knowing he'd have some alone time. His real name was
Jan Gunnar Sorensen. His father took tremendous pride
in their Norse heritage and wanted the world to know
what type of stalk they came from. "Jan" seemed like a
decent enough name until fifth grade. The other boys'
interpretation of Jan meant "boy with a girl's name," so
he started going by Gunnar. As he got older and started to
take up hunting, people just assumed that guns were his
thing, so the spelling and pronunciation sadly changed to
Gunner. He really didn't care. It was just a nickname to
him anyway.

The disciplined hunter had been tracking the
relatively unfamiliar territory for a good forty minutes
now. He was close. Gunner laid his gun against a massive
tree and pulled a special set of binoculars from his bag.
He also pulled a bottle that contained a deer musk scent,
which was reapplied quite liberally to himself and the
surrounding area. The gag-inducing smell always made
him nauseous, but he took a couple of deep breaths
through his mouth and tried to calm his mind.

Gunner lifted the binoculars and combed the
seemingly lifeless landscape. If memory served correctly,
a small stream flowed about a half mile to the north, so
he searched the hilly terrain to the east just ahead. After
a few sweeps, he found what he was looking for about
two hundred yards from where he sat: a small opening
to a den he had scouted a few weeks earlier. A slight rush
of adrenaline gave a jolt to his heart, but he trusted his
instincts and waited perfectly still.

* * *

During one of his annual trips to stock up on

firewood for the winter, Gunner had stopped on the side of the road to fix one of the tarp straps that covered the logs. It had been just before dusk, and the breeze was swirling the leaves around the ditch. One of them rose like a flimsy paper airplane and caught Gunner square in the eye.

The sting made him venture off the side of the road toward the edge of the forest to get away from the wind and swirling debris. He let his eye swell with water for a few minutes, and then he cleared the pesky fragments from his face. When he looked up, he locked eyes with the beast for only a brief second. Even with the sun fading over the horizon and an agitated eye, he had known exactly what he was seeing. During what seemed like a millisecond, Gunner's memory took a photograph and burned it into his brain. A wild gray wolf had stood in front of a fallen tree about fifty yards from where the man had been standing, an unmistakably defunct calf in its mouth. Before Gunner could react, the wolf had eerily disappeared without making a sound, as if disintegrating into the wind.

Throughout the rest of the drive home, the gears in Gunner's brain had been running at Mach 3. He just couldn't extinguish the image of the wolf from his head. That one picture had served as the perfect surveillance photo as if a private detective had hand-delivered it in a manilla folder.

First, the wolf had been alone. That in and of itself didn't mean very much. It could have easily meant that Gunner didn't see the rest of the pack, or the wolf had been caught scouting the area, or any other number of possible scenarios. Second, the fact that it had a dead calf in its mouth denoted that the wolf had been hunting. Wolves usually hunt in packs at night, and it would be highly unlikely that one of them would venture off by itself with a fresh kill almost entirely intact. Third, the prey says a lot about the hunter. The calf had probably been grazing with a herd of cattle nearby. Wolves don't typically hunt cattle unless their food supply is scarce and they have limited options. It does happen, but not as often as most people think. Their fear of humans is quite considerable. Which brings us to the fourth fact: Gunner had seen the wolf with a fresh kill at only about 150 strides away. Any healthy wild gray wolf would not wander that close to a human. Wolves are highly elusive, and their sense of hearing makes it almost impossible to sneak up on them even while they are asleep.

Something must have been wrong with this particular wolf. The most likely scenario was that it had some form of disease or illness. Wolves usually leave the pack when this happens in order to protect the others. The problem is they are better hunters as a pack. The illness that this lone wolf was most likely suffering from was affecting its hearing, so hunting other wild animals was on the brink of impossible. Desperation was probably why it had resorted to hunting grazing cattle during daylight hours.

Gunner had spent the next few weeks scoping the area and asking around to see if there were any recently documented livestock attacks. Aside from the usual foxes and badgers roaming the area, no one had seen or heard of any wolves on the prowl. In fact, none of the local ranchers had even reported any missing calves. If

Gunner's instincts were correct, the wolf had just started preying on livestock.

* * *

Black clouds took the moon hostage for a few silent minutes. Gunner sat astonishingly still within a gnarled thicket of branches, the tip of his gun aimed through a small opening. His legs were a little stiff, and his neck felt like a brick had been dropped on it, but nothing was going to deter him from this avocation. He waited for the clouds to release what was left of the moon before he lifted the binoculars back to his eyes. Still no sign of his feather in cap.

This kind of opportunity only presents itself in a once-in-a-lifetime sort of way. The mysterious animal had probably developed a taste for cattle, and it was becoming increasingly less intimidated by humans. It wouldn't be long before DNR was on its trail to capture and destroy it. They tended to do that with desperate and dangerous game. Gunner was just doing everyone a favor, even though the law wasn't in one hundred percent agreement.

The sun would be coming up soon. He would have to be on his way back before his wife woke up to an empty bed. A warm bead of perspiration dripped onto his steady hand. He calmly wiped it onto the side of his pants. With the gun perched in the crook of his arm, Gunner meticulously shifted his weight from one foot to the other and used his free arm to wipe the sweat from his forehead. He rubbed his eyes for a few seconds, letting the sting from fatigue and sweat slowly dissolve. A soft breeze rattled his eardrums as his eyes readjusted to the thin sliver of orange on the horizon.

The unwavering hunter put the binoculars back up to his eyes. His blood froze, and his body tensed. Something moved in front of the den. The binoculars were now a part of his body as he trained them like a laser on the narrow location in the distance. The breeze may have been playing tricks on his eyes. All Gunner could see was the black tree branches gently swaying back and forth. He didn't blink for nearly two minutes. Waiting.

Maybe it was just the breeze. He was scared to even breathe, just in case. As he gently allowed himself to exhale, the breeze began to die down, and the branches fell to rest. Within the protection of darkness and the ever-shifting shadows, two faint yellow glowing eyes emerged like embers in a dying campfire.

In one efficient motion, Gunner replaced the binoculars with the scope of his gun. He could see the entire outline of the animal. He lined the crosshairs just below its front leg, in the area of the heart. His finger found its way to the trigger as he applied mild pressure. He took one deep breath, held it for half a second, and then breathed out and relaxed the barrel of the gun in his firmly outstretched hand. He pulled the trigger the rest of the way, and a deafening shot left the familiar ringing in his ears.

The wolf flew backwards and dropped to the forest floor immediately. Gunner breathed a sigh of relief because he knew his aim was true, and the animal didn't suffer. As he looked through the scope of his gun, he could see that the animal was not moving. It had suffered enough already.

Even though this was an act of mercy in the young

man's eyes, the law wouldn't view it in the same light. He decided to wait before going to retrieve the kill, just to be absolutely sure nobody else was in the area. The last thing he needed was to have to try and explain himself to Johnny Lawman. People that lived in a black and white world just wouldn't be able to understand.

The forest was still silent as dawn began to vanquish its shadows. Gunner read 6:09 on his watch. It would take him about forty minutes to get back to his SUV by himself, closer to an hour with the body draped over his shoulders. He decided he would wait ten more minutes before going to collect his kill.

He carefully strapped his gun over his shoulder and collected his things. Before putting his binoculars in his bag, the hunter decided to sweep the area one last time. He scanned through the trees to the south and then over to the west, the direction he had come. Nothing important was moving. He scanned to the north near the stream and found nothing. He decided the coast was clear and went to gather the body.

The journey back to the SUV was harder than expected. Gunner had to stop twice to readjust his gun strap. The sun had peaked its head up by the time he made it back to the rendezvous point. He laid his kill behind the back of the vehicle and searched for his keys. It took him several moments before he found them in his binocular bag. Out of paranoia, he used the binoculars to sweep the remote area, just to be safe. Nothing was moving behind to the east or to the south. He quickly looked west and then to the north. He felt a pit in his stomach as movement caught his eye.

Way off in the distance in an opening through the trees about three hundred yards out, Gunner saw a hunched-over figure dragging something through the grass near the stream. What the hell was it? The thing doing the dragging had to be a person. Gunner squinted hard through the binoculars and slightly moved his head back and forth as if willing the shadows and massive tree trunks to dance around and let the morning light be used as a spotlight.

It was definitely a person pulling a large indeterminate object with what looked to be a rope. Gunner couldn't quite make out exactly what it was, but the person looked to be expending a lot of energy pulling it. Could someone else have been out poaching this morning? He was sure the only gunshot he'd heard was his own. This person was dragging something in the opposite direction, so Gunner couldn't get a glimpse of the face. Slowly but surely, whoever it was was welcomed back into the arms of the forest and disappeared out of sight. Gunner didn't want to wait around to find out who they were or what they were doing, so he decided to just leave it alone. He had more important things to attend to.

The hunter quickly packed up his things, placed the wolf's body in the back of his vehicle, and drove off in the opposite direction with the lights off for a quarter mile. He was feeling a little bit exposed but not panicked just yet. He had to get back home and hide the evidence in case anyone caught his license plate.

* * *

Jamie kicked the sheets off her legs. The cool air felt refreshing on her bare skin. She could feel the heat trying to escape like steam evaporating from a boiling pot. Her throat felt like it was coated in dust every time she tried to swallow. She must have forgotten to gulp down a large glass of water before curling up next to the body pillow on her edge of the bed.

Her fingers brushed a few tangled strands of blonde hair out of her face as she reached across the nightstand to pull the dim glow of her digital clock closer to her face. The numbers were fuzzy, but she squinted long enough to make out 5:03 in large block numbers. The young woman could already feel the slight twinge of pain beginning to pulsate in her forehead. She closed her eyes and laid there for a few minutes, contemplating if she should make the effort to go downstairs and rehydrate. The thought of leaving the comfort of a warm bed was unbearable, especially if she had to wander around in the darkness.

Jan had already been in bed for who knows how long by the time Jamie had come upstairs around two or so. Or was it later? He may or may not have been sleeping, but she was sure he had been awake by the time she finally fell into bed. Jan hadn't said anything when she got under the covers. He had just laid on his side of the bed facing the bedroom door. She knew he was awake because he usually stirred and rolled over when he was rudely plucked from the ever-elusive dreamland, but tonight he hadn't moved.

Jamie had tried to wait for him to drift off because she liked to focus on the sound of his steady heavy breathing, but she must have fallen asleep first. That seemed to be happening more often than not lately. If she got up to grab a glass of water right now, it would probably just wake him up again and give him another reason to be pissed off.

Jamie could feel her body start to ease its way back into a dream, but her head kept reminding her that she would pay for it later if she didn't get up right now. She opened one eye and stared out the window into the empty blackness. The sun would be up soon. Maybe if she just laid here long enough, she could wait for the comforting rays of sunshine to light her path to the kitchen.

The young woman shifted her gaze under the window to where she thought the electrical outlet might have been. She had insisted a few times that they plug some night lights into the unused outlets, but Jan always complained that he needed complete darkness to get a good nights' sleep. He refused to wear any kind of mask over his face either. He said he couldn't get used to wearing something on his face while he slept. So Jamie usually made sure her phone was plugged into the outlet near her nightstand in case she had to get up to use the bathroom or something. She glanced at the spot where she usually put it, but she must have left it downstairs on the kitchen counter before she came to bed.

Jamie could still taste that third shot of cheap whiskey underneath the toothpaste. She had reluctantly slammed it at the behest of her friend, Allie, right before their Lyft had shown up to drive them home from the bar. They had gone out to meet some coworkers for a drink after their shift had ended at the clinic and ended up nearly closing the place down. Jamie remembered the ride home but couldn't remember if she had laid her phone on the kitchen counter next to her keys when she attempted to gracefully slip in the back door.

The thought of feeling her way through the darkness

made her pull the covers back over her bare legs. She was sure she was probably sweating through her favorite pair of green shorts, but she still felt a shiver run through her legs. She promised herself just a few more minutes, and then she would make herself get up and go down to the kitchen.

Jamie closed her eyes and listened for the sound of her husband's rhythmic breathing to lull her back to sleep, but there was no sound coming from his side of the bed. She carefully moved her elbow behind her, hoping to gently make contact with Jan's back, but all she felt was a crumpled sheet and a cool pillow. She rolled over and put her hand on the empty space of his side of the bed. He must have gotten up and gone downstairs. Maybe he couldn't get back to sleep. That probably meant he would be pissed off.

Jamie just sighed and pulled the covers tightly over her whole body. She wrapped her arm around her large body pillow and snuggled it close to her face. The twinge of pain in her head intensified as her heart pounded a little bit faster. The last thought that drifted through her mind before she fell back to sleep was that tomorrow morning was probably going to suck.

CHAPTER TWO

Gunner sat in the safety of his detached garage staring at the clock on the dashboard of his SUV — 7:40. He had a difficult decision to make: quickly skin the wolf hide so he wouldn't have to worry about bacteria rendering it useless, or cover his tracks and duck into the house to check on his wife.

He looked through the rearview mirror that caught a reflection of the two-story country house and then behind his seat at the lump under the blanket. "Sorry, but you're going to have to stay hidden just a little bit longer," he whispered toward the blanket. Better to be safe than sorry at this point.

The young hunter hit the garage door button and silently crept over the driveway and onto the lawn, being especially mindful of leaves and other potentially loud debris. The air was perfectly crisp when it touched his face, sparking reminiscence of caramel apples and hayrides of his youth. This just added fuel to his already simmering excitement. The usually stoic man almost skipped the rest of the way into the house. He slid inside and quietly closed the door while taking off his shoes.

His wife tended to be a bit of a night owl, but she slept soundly once finally in bed. She was in bed around

1:30 last night, earlier than most Friday nights. The two used to go out and party quite a bit when they were first married, but Gunner eventually needed to make a choice about which relationship suited him best: the one with his wife, Jamie, or the one with Jack Daniels. He decided Jack just couldn't love him back, so the two parted ways.

As he methodically avoided every little creaky floorboard as if they would set off a land mine, Gunner realized he hadn't used the bathroom since he snuck out of the house in the middle of the night. He went through the kitchen, bypassed the stairway to their bedroom, and went into the half bathroom. It was beside the great room where the fire had almost died. He flicked on the light, and before he could close the door, the young man noticed the hand towel was damp. There were specks of water in the sink too. Gunner's excitement immediately began to fizzle.

What was he going to tell his wife if she noticed he wasn't in bed or on the couch? *Dammit!* he thought to himself. *Why didn't I stop and get bagels or doughnuts or something on the way back? I could have had an alibi.*

He reached into his pocket and looked at his phone. No calls or unread texts. Maybe she was too out of it to notice he wasn't there. But why did she use the downstairs bathroom? She was probably in there no more than twenty minutes ago, hopefully. He could just say he couldn't sleep and decided to go get some firewood from the garage.

After he finished up in the bathroom, Gunner went upstairs to their bedroom with no real plan in mind. He peeked his head into the room and found Jamie lying on her side of the bed, seemingly in a deep slumber. Her breathing was slow and heavy. Gunner waited in the doorway for a few minutes. He was deciding how he would deal with his whereabouts if it came up later. As he stood and watched her, he noticed that she seemed pretty out of it.

As far as he was concerned, he hadn't really done anything wrong at this point. But if he told her the truth, that he was out poaching a wolf, she would probably get upset about it. She never understood the whole hunting thing, especially the part about being alone in the woods waiting to kill a defenseless animal. She sure as hell wouldn't understand poaching a majestic grey wolf. It wasn't in her nature. So Gunner would just avoid the issue altogether and hope nobody would find out. He thought about the wolf pelt sitting in the back of his SUV. He should really take care of that while the coast was clear.

The husband gently closed the bedroom door and went straight to the garage. He opened the side door this time and pulled out his phone. He searched "how to skin a wolf" on his browser. He had a pretty good idea of how to do it because he had been hunting wild game ever since he was old enough to shoot a gun, but he wanted some notes from people who had done it firsthand. A website came up that was more of a message board containing posts from hunters in Alaska. It was a rather primitive site that seemed to be a way for them to share ideas about hunting. Sure enough, Gunner came across a couple of posts about skinning wolves.

It looked like the best way to save the fur was to start the cut from the inside. That was the case with most big game furs if the hunter wanted to reduce hair trimmings on the meat. Gunner read a few more posts that said roughly the same thing, then closed his phone and went over to his bench to grab his cutting utensils. He opened the back of the SUV and carefully pulled the body out of the blanket. The wolf's temperature had dropped a bit, but it was still warm from being under the blanket. It was time to go to work, but it would have to be done in the shed, the small unit that sat alone down on the edge of the tree line in the backyard. The decrepit structure creeped Jamie out, and she had aptly named it the "Slaughterhouse."

* * *

Gunner met Jamie shortly after his father, Fredrick, had become very ill. Gunner was nineteen and had come home from his job in Detroit when he heard his father was in the hospital because of a rare blood disease. The son had been in the hospital visiting his father one night, and the two got into a heated argument about Fredrick's stubbornness to not go to the doctor sooner. The doctor had explained that by the time Fredrick was finally in enough pain to go to the hospital, the disease had progressed significantly.

Gunner got angry and needed to go somewhere to blow off some steam. He irritably left the hospital and went to a dive bar where he knew the bouncer would let him in, even though IDs were supposed to be checked at the door. The two were mutual acquaintances from high school who had run into each other at a party or two back in the day, but that was enough for the bouncer to know he wouldn't cause any trouble. Gunner never really needed to be the center of attention, and he often liked to observe before participating in social gatherings.

On this particular night, the social gathering was an especially crowded bar. The fall college semester had started back up, and people were in the mood to rekindle their friendships. The packed bar happened to make Gunner a little anxious, more so than usual.

He decided to grab a seat near a small table toward the dimly lit back wall. A jumbled mess of dollar bills that had been defaced with colorful ink and crude drawings were glued to the unique wall. Gunner smirked at some of the drawings before throwing his leather jacket over the rickety chair and weaving his way through clusters of similar-aged young adults back to the bar. He expeditiously ordered two Jack Cokes and brought them straight back to his isolated table in the corner of the dingy bar.

As he chugged the first one, all he could think about was his father's criticism at the hospital. "That jacket makes you look like a punk," and "If you can't grow a full beard, then why do you have any facial hair at all?," not to mention the tattoos and "paltry" gages in his ear lobes.

Why couldn't his father just accept him for who he was? It frustrated Gunner even more so tonight because he had taken time off from his new job in Detroit to drive back home. If his father didn't want to see him, then he should have said so over the phone. It would have saved him time and money on gas and food.

After Gunner slammed his second drink, he sat at his undersized table seething for a few minutes. He was debating if he should go back to the hospital, back to Detroit, or just get annihilated and figure out the rest later. His father had made it perfectly clear that he wanted to be left alone in his boring isolated wing of the hospital, so the least Gunner could do was honor his wish, even if it was laced with a few drops of spite.

The volume of the place seemed to get turned up about twenty decibels in the brief amount of time Gunner had been sulking in the corner. The music had gradually changed from grungy dive bar music to a more upbeat bass-rattling hip hop mix, so people had started to crowd toward the middle of the bar to sway their hips while they yelled at each other between sips of their drinks. The chaotic blender of noise made it impossible to think clearly, so the agitated young man decided it was time for more drinks. If anything, he could catch a nice buzz before his spot in the corner was usurped by a group of douchebag frat boys looking to creep on the talent.

Gunner grabbed his jacket off the chair and slung it over his shoulder as he tried to navigate his way back up to the flustered bartender. As he slid and grinded his way between tightly packed bodies, he saw two guys wearing polo shirts, and backwards Tigers caps pounce on the lonely table in the corner. "Pfft, fucking figures," Gunner muttered to himself.

As he turned back toward the bar, he accidentally bumped into a pretty blonde and made her drop her drink. The plastic cup splattered ice and some kind of pink sticky liquid all over the floor. Luckily the music was so loud, and the bar was so dim that few people seemed to notice what had happened.

"I'm so sorry," yelled Gunner. He could barely even hear himself. He almost decided to just duck and run before she had a chance to react, but for some reason, he couldn't look away from her.

"It's totally okay. I was almost done with it anyway," she yelled back. Maybe it was the lighting, but it looked like she was barely wearing any makeup. Her pure white teeth cut through the darkness as a smile formed across her face. Her eyes darted down to the tattoos on Gunner's forearms.

"Let me buy you another one," he yelled. "It's the least I can do for being such a jackass." Normally he would have muttered an apology and bounced as soon as he could to save himself the embarrassment, but he had pounded those mixed drinks so fast his head was swimming.

She replied, "Only if you and your friends come have a drink with me and my girls."

Gunner paused a moment before responding. He was deciding if he really wanted to be alone that night. There was something about this girl that was alluring. He would have to make up a story if he was going to go over to her table because she would think he was a degenerate or an alcoholic if he was in the bar by himself.

"I was actually just going to pay the tab. My friends ditched me at the moment for another bar," he yelled.

She yelled back, "That's okay, you can meet up with them in a bit. You still owe me a drink anyway. My name's Jamie."

"Okay, they can wait. My name's Jan, but most people call me Gunner."

* * *

After about an hour of intense work, Gunner emerged from the slaughterhouse wiping his hands on a dark cloth. He had used some old coveralls and a black plastic apron to keep the blood from getting all over his clothes. The meat was hastily wrapped and thrown in a confined freezer that sat in the shed. The hunter was intrigued by the thought of tasting wolf for the first time, but he wanted to make sure he prepared it the right way. He didn't know how many other opportunities would ever present themselves like this one.

It had to be mid-morning by now, so Gunner walked into the garage and tossed the used cloth on the work bench. He then loaded his arms with a few pieces of dry firewood. He didn't want to go back into the house empty-handed this time, even though the sun had warmed the air enough to make him want to take off his gray hoodie.

When Gunner finally got to the back door and opened it with his foot, the smell of fresh ground coffee immediately invaded his nose. Jamie was up and probably hung over. It was the only time she ever made coffee. There was a steady black stream that had filled half the pot so far. The miniature TV that hung underneath the cabinets was on at a low volume too. There was some news story about a local girl or something. Gunner ignored it and walked to the front of the house near the fireplace.

Jamie was sitting on the couch playing with her phone. She looked up with tired eyes and simply said, "Hey."

Gunner replied, "Hey. You just get up?"

She was busy typing something on her phone. She mumbled, "Kind of. I laid in bed for a bit with a headache, but I think I just need some food."

She didn't seem to be acting overly suspicious. In fact, she didn't even ask Gunner what he had been doing just now. He thought about asking her when exactly she woke up but decided not to draw attention to the matter. He feared the inevitable conversation of his whereabouts would surface, so he tried to steer the conversation somewhere else.

"You want me to run and get some bagels or something?" he asked.

Jamie sighed and looked out the window for a second. "Yeah, if you don't mind. I feel like shit, and some comfort food might help. Can you get the ones with the blueberries?"

Gunner responded, "Yeah, I'll be back in a bit," and went straight for the door.

* * *

Jamie looked up from her phone just as her husband scurried out the back door. She heard the SUV start and watched it back down the driveway from the front window. At least he actually spoke to her this morning. There was nothing worse than dreading the angry silence that couldn't be filled with a blaring TV channel or percolating coffee.

The tired woman got up from the couch and wandered into the kitchen. She went straight for the medicine cabinet and rattled a couple of ibuprofen from the tiny bottle. She filled a glass of water to the brim and drowned the pills in her stomach. This stupid headache was not going to ruin her Saturday.

Jamie looked at her phone screen and noticed a series of text messages from Allie.

Omg shouldn't have t8kn those shots b4 getting a ride last night

Pretty sure I gave my digits to the driver lol
How was Jan this morning?

Jamie put her thumbs up to the tiny keyboard but hesitated before typing a response. She didn't quite know how to answer. Something just seemed off this morning. Jan wasn't quite angry, more like dismissive. Maybe her headache was clouding her intuition.

As she started to walk back toward the couch, her big toe jammed into a stiff piece of firewood and sent it rolling across the floor. A sharp pain resonated through her foot.

"Owww! Shit!!" she yelled as she bent down to massage the pain away. Jan must have just left the wood sitting near the table instead of bringing it into the front room. What was the point of leaving it here if the fire was in there? Sometimes he could be so careless when his mind was focused on something else.

Jamie slowly bent down and picked up the logs. She was amazed she hadn't dropped her phone and put another dent in it. At least it wouldn't have been her fault this time. She placed the phone on the table and cradled the three logs in her arms.

As she walked to the front of the house, Jamie felt a bit of a chill run up her back. She set the logs down in the wicker basket next to the couch and opened the glass door to the fireplace. The glass was surprisingly cool to the touch. A few red embers sat smoldering in a pile of gray ash, and the wind echoed through the shaft that led up through the chimney. Jan almost never let the fire go out, especially on a Saturday morning when he was up so early.

Jamie picked up an old paper bag they used for burning scraps and tore a few shreds. She crumpled them up and gently placed them on what was left of a smoldering piece of charred wood. The paper began to contort against the heat. She then reached into the bottom of the wicker basket, dug out some small pieces of bark and sticks, and scattered them over the paper. As the paper began to billow smoke, she carefully blew on the bottom of the pile while being mindful not to send hot ash ricocheting into her delicate face.

After a few minutes of fanning the smoldering scraps, a small yellow flame leapt up from the bottom of the pile. Jamie took a second to revel in her accomplishment but also to keep from falling over from the resounding pain in her head. Fanning the flame had left her feeling a bit nauseous and lightheaded. Keeping the fire going was supposed to be Jan's job.

The annoyed young woman tossed the remaining three logs on the fire and closed the glass door. She was confident it would keep going, at least until her husband returned. She then walked back to the kitchen, grabbed her phone, and started typing a reply to Allie as she came back to the couch.

Idk. He was hiding out somewhere all morning.

Jamie could feel the heat of the fire start to warm the room. She closed her eyes and laid her head back on the soft fabric of the couch. She felt tired but had already overslept. There was no point in trying to fall back asleep.

An acrid aroma of coffee started to meld into the subtle smell of smoke in the room. Maybe a big cup of coffee would jolt her awake. Hopefully, Jan would be back with food soon. She hated drinking coffee on an empty stomach. It always made her nerves feel like they were dangerously close to suffering a panic attack.

The phone buzzed, and a message from Allie popped onto the screen.

Up to old habits?

Jamie put the phone down and closed her eyes again. That's not what she had meant to insinuate. Jan was probably just being sulky because she had stayed out later than she had initially planned. She had meant to text him last night, but she didn't want him to be mad at her. She feared getting a brazen response, or worse, nothing at all. Besides, it was his choice to stay home.

It was easier when he used to come along for the ride, but those nights were beginning to feel like a distant memory. They used to sleep in together until mid-morning, just to wake up long enough to eventually stumble their way down to the couch. They would lie there basking in the morning sunshine and argue over whose turn it was to go get a pile of greasy food to soak up the residual effects from the previous night. They had even resorted to childish games of rock, paper, scissors on more than one occasion, but best of three would turn into best of five, and so on. It was a battle of attrition that she usually won because Jan would succumb to hunger, but she usually folded and accompanied him to town anyway.

Maybe things really did change when people approached their thirties. She always knew they couldn't live the lifestyles of a couple of kids in their early twenties forever, but things seemed to change so drastically over the last few years. Being married at twenty-two had seemed like such a great idea at the time, but maybe the decision was just as impulsive as every other one they made at that age. Who really knows themselves at twenty-two?

Jamie opened her eyes and picked up her phone again. The throbbing in her head was finally starting to subside. She hastily texted a response to Allie.

I don't think so?

CHAPTER THREE

The young Sorensen couple lived just a few miles outside of the official city limits. It seemed more remote than it actually was because Gunner drove by a large pumpkin patch and a couple of half barren seas of golden corn stalks. The crops were in full harvest as people worked overtime to get as much work as possible done before the sun eluded them on the Upper Michigan Peninsula. In fact, the town was getting ready for its annual fall celebration. Most of the roughly fifty-thousand residents participated in one way or another.

Gunner used to use the celebration as just another excuse to get shit-faced drunk, but sobriety had a way of making him become a little bit more open-minded. In recent years, spiced apple cider had become a guilty pleasure. Making an appearance at the carnival was also a new trend. In his youth, the hunter would never have set foot in or around anything involving carnivals or circuses. Last year was the first time he finally gave in to Jamie's constant harassment. As a result, Gunner found out that the carnival was nothing like the summer fair booths that contained rigged games and deep-fried food. It was geared more toward a jumbled theme of harvest reaping, old folk stories, and Halloween. Every year, as the growing season came to an end, the once fruitful fields became tilled, and the trees said goodbye to their leaves, the town ironically came to life with jubilant celebration.

As the SUV whizzed past the green population sign, it was as if civilization magically appeared over the hill. Serene forests and reposed fields were replaced by neon lights and drab-colored business buildings. The trendy coffee shop bakery that Gunner was heading toward was located on the north side of town, but he decided he wanted to check out the main strip where most of the celebration was about to take place. The SUV turned off the highway and took a detour through the quaint old district downtown.

The man drove by building after building that had signs about deals for the upcoming Harvest Moon Fall Festival. He also drove past the park that sat in the middle of what used to be called Town Square. It was actually a gazebo with a few walking paths, picnic benches, and some nicely trimmed trees. On this particular day, though, the park had been transformed with large tents lined with hay bales and corn stalks. The tents were long and resembled a similar layout to the Oktoberfest tents in Germany. There was also an unusually large amount of people gathered around the park, even for this time of year.

Gunner wondered if some new theme or exhibit was coming to town this year, so he decided to find a parking spot down the street and walk back to where the action seemed to be. The downtown district embodied the charm of Main Street America, where Mom and Pop stores still reigned supreme. The historic two-story brick buildings were lined next to each other in neat and uniform rows, some with black awnings hanging over the sidewalk. There were antique shops, bookstores, restaurants, and even a taffy store on the main strip. A popular zoning ordinance had kept the commercial and corporate chains from penetrating the downtown district.

As he walked the few blocks back toward the crowd that had gathered in Town Square, he began to feel an uneasy tension that gripped the air. People were standing around either fixated on their phones or on the person speaking toward the front of the gathering. Gunner edged his way toward the back of the crowd, but he still couldn't quite see what exactly was taking place. He stood on his toes to try and peek over the heads of the people in front of him, and by doing so, he caught a glimpse of the sunglasses that belonged to the man doing the talking. The conspicuous sunglasses sat on top of the head of Paul Stansby, Chief of Police.

The officer had the crowd in the palm of his hand while he spoke with a bellowing voice. He looked like he could have been the ringmaster for a Ringling Brothers Circus in a previous life. He was just finishing his speech, saying, "If you have any information regarding her whereabouts, please don't hesitate to come forward. Thank you." That's all Gunner heard as the crowd began to dissipate.

He looked around to see if he could find any clue as to what the hell Officer Stansby was talking about. When he couldn't figure it out right away, he started to get anxious. Then he just sort of grabbed the first guy that walked past him and asked, "What was that guy talking about?"

The guy being grabbed was probably in his mid-thirties and had his wife holding onto his other arm. The man looked startled, and kind of took a step back.

"Sorry, I just heard the tail end of the speech. What was the officer talking about?" asked Gunner.

The man looked at his wife for a second as if silently asking her for permission. Then he looked up and said, "A jogger went missing. He was just asking if people had any information about her. That's all."

Gunner simply replied, "Thanks." Then he began to scour the area for a possible photo of the missing girl. Sure enough, there was a picture of a young brunette on the front of the podium. She couldn't have been much younger than Gunner, probably mid-twenties. She was wearing a purple sweatshirt and sitting in the grass, her hand tugging at her long hair. Her face was sort of tilted to one side with her lips pursed into a shy smile like the camera had caught her in a personal moment.

People began to float by Gunner as they headed toward their vehicles, so he allowed his thoughts to drift with them. He had never seen this girl before today. He probably would have remembered her. She wasn't the most beautiful girl he had ever seen, but her eyes seemed to have a genuineness that can rarely be faked. He would have noticed her, even if only from a glance.

Gunner stood there a while longer, wondering how long this girl had been missing. It had to have been at least a few days if everyone was starting to form search parties and organize rallies in the middle of town. Now that the cops were involved, it must be quite serious. But even so, in today's society, everyone freaked out if you didn't respond to a text right away or reply to an email or IM in a timely manner. With GPS in our cars and on our phones, it seemed very difficult for anybody to just fall off the side of the earth. Gunner, of all people, would definitely understand if the girl wanted to get away from it all for a brief amount of time, but she would have to be extremely committed if she was trying to remain isolated. Something must have happened.

Gunner suddenly snapped back to reality and remembered why he had come to town in the first place: bagels. As he started for his vehicle, he had the feeling that a keen pair of eyes were on him. He glanced toward the side of the podium and saw Officer Stansby standing in the shadow with his arms crossed. His eyes were shielded under his sunglasses, but Gunner had a hunch that they might be cast his way. The young hunter pretended like he didn't notice and continued walking back to his SUV.

* * *

It was five years ago when Gunner sat hunched on the edge of the sidewalk, his legs sprawled over the curb and resting in the street. He had to squint his eyes because the constant flashing of red and blue lights was giving him a headache. His head was spinning, and his hand was throbbing underneath a blood-soaked bandage. Shattered glass lay strewn all over the sidewalk behind him.

Officer Stansby's authoritative voice could be heard from down the block. "And was anything stolen?"

The man standing next to him was the owner of one of the local antique stores. He cocked his head to the side and mumbled something to the officer. He threw Gunner a disapproving shake of the head and then went back to speaking just out of earshot.

The lights were off in all the shops except for the antique store. The strip along Main Street was hauntingly quiet, the only car being a police cruiser shining its lights on Gunner's little transgression. Refractions of red and blue glimmered in the broken glass in front of the store entrance.

When Stansby was finished taking the man's statement, he made a beeline back to where the young man sat. "Well, kid, the store owner is a pretty understanding man. He says he's sorry to hear about your father, but he's willing to not press charges if you return the wooden figurine and go apologize. He'll just send you the bill for his window."

Gunner sat and stared at the ground before giving a vehement response. "He's not supposed to take a gift and sell it for profit! My dad carved those damn things himself. He also gave them to that guy thinking they would be put in a display case, not stuck in the front window with a price tag on them!"

Officer Stansby immediately replied, "As far as I'm concerned, you're sitting in the street piss drunk with a bandage wrapped around your hand. I get called here at two-thirty in the morning to investigate property damage and theft, so I'm running out of patience. Those figurines were in that man's possession, so he can do whatever he damn well pleases with them! Now either you give them back and apologize, or I can just haul your ass to detox for the rest of the weekend. Maybe even county jail if the man decides he wants to press charges. It's your choice, kid."

Gunner closed his eyes for a second, contemplating

his options. He was being given a real life get-out-of-jail-free card. He was caught red-handed, literally, stealing from a local establishment and vandalizing property. This was a no-brainer decision. Then he thought about all the time his father had spent carving those stupid things and how he just gave them away to someone who was supposed to be somewhat of a friend.

Gunner took the figurine out of his pocket and twirled it in his fingers. The memory of his father sitting in his chair flicking pieces of wood on the table flooded his brain, so he impulsively smashed the figurine on the curb. That was the last thing he remembered before waking up in county jail the next day.

* * *

The trendy bakery lived up to its reputation on this eventful morning. It seemed like every college kid that wasn't sleeping off the previous night's affairs was in there. Gunner used his foot to gently kick the glass door open so he could bring a handful of bagels, doughnuts, and raspberry cream back to his vehicle. He half walked, half jogged so the anxiety wouldn't asphyxiate him.

He slammed the car door shut, put both hands on the wheel, and slowly let out a deep sigh. *WAY too many people in such an enclosed space*, he thought to himself. He took a moment to look at himself in the rearview mirror. He noticed the black bags under his eyes and the red streak under his chin. Gunner wiped the streak onto his hand and brought it up to his nose to smell it. It kind of smelled like raspberry. Or was that from the bag he had just thrown onto the passenger seat? He wasn't about to taste the streak under his chin, so he just wiped it on a napkin he pulled from the glove compartment.

The young man peeked in the bag and noticed that one of the raspberry packets was leaking all over. He must have stuck the bag under his chin when he attempted to pay and run out of the bakery. At least it wasn't all over his seats...yet.

Gunner decided he didn't want to head back through town on his way out, so he took the back streets that led to one of the main highways. He turned onto the entrance ramp and quickly got his vehicle up to speed. The sky had transformed to a dreary gray haze that was slightly lighter than the weather-beaten asphalt on the road. The hum of the tires made Gunner's frazzled brain start to fire on multiple cylinders, making it difficult to focus on one thought at a time. He tried to center his attention on the missing woman. The consensus seemed to be that she had gone for a jog and never came back. There weren't a lot of hiking trails around the area, so she probably would have had to stick to roads and sidewalks. If she were injured running in those locations, somebody would have found her by now. So maybe she was abducted, but that seemed a bit far-fetched because of the amount of traffic around these parts. Even if she was jogging on a gravel road, there weren't too many stretches with a lack of houses. There was very little chance she would go trouncing through the gnarled thicket of forest unless she wandered way out—

Blip bleep!!

The man's meager amount of concentration was rudely interrupted by the short wail of a police siren. Gunner looked behind him and noticed the distinct grill of a police car closely tailing him. *Dammit! Now what?* he thought to himself. He pulled the vehicle over, reached into his back pocket to pull out his wallet, and waited for presumably Officer Stansby to approach his window.

The officer slowly crept alongside the SUV before presenting herself at the driver's window. It was Stansby's deputy, Officer Mary Renard. Her light brown ponytail dangled above the navy-blue collar of her uniform.

She rapped on the window with her knuckle, her other hand placed firmly on her hip. She had a hard-line steely look, probably from overcompensating for her callow face and having to constantly prove herself as a young woman in an authoritative position. Gunner had seen her around but never had any interactions with her until now. He wasn't sure what to expect as he rolled down the window.

"License, please," she said as sternly as she could. Gunner obliged and handed it to her. He wondered how she looked twenty-five but sounded forty.

She narrowed her deadpan eyes to study it for a good minute before cutting right to the chase and saying, "I pulled you over because of your cracked windshield."

Gunner looked at the pea-sized rock indent and the corresponding two to three inches of a hairline crack that was just beginning to crawl across the driver's side of the glass. He thought to himself, *Is there such a thing as being a bit too nit-picky?*

As if reading his thoughts, Officer Renard quickly replied, "I know it's not very big right now, but it can still obstruct your vision." She turned his driver's license over and studied the back. "I'm not gonna give you a ticket, but I am going to need you to take care of that ASAP."

Gunner just responded by saying, "Thank you, I'll do it as soon as I can." He held out his hand and waited for her to give his license back. "Is there something else?"

Officer Renard looked at him and said, "I see you've got your firearm safety. Do you have a conceal and carry permit?"

Gunner never had someone ask him about that before. "No, I don't even own a pistol," he replied.

Ms. Renard flipped the license over and handed it back to the young man. Then she started peering into the back of the SUV and asked, "You wouldn't have any concealed weapons back there, would you, Mr. Sorensen? Considering you don't have a conceal and carry permit of any kind, that is."

Gunner gave her a weird "why do you ask?" kind of look before responding, "No, I usually keep my rifle in my garage or house unless I'm hunting. Then I leave it in its case if it's being transported."

He looked in the back just to make sure. All that was back there was a bloody blanket. He was positive he hadn't left a rifle or a black case back there. There may have been a few stray bullet casings hiding under the blanket, but that was it.

"Oh, it kind of looked like you might have done some hunting recently. I just figured it would be in your best interest to let me know if there was a gun under that blanket."

"No gun," Gunner simply replied. "Can I go now?"

Officer Renard gave him a coy smile and said, "Yeah, we're done here."

* * *

Jamie was still lying on the couch in the front room of the empty house. She was listening to music on her phone and lazily scrolling through her Facebook feed. She would alternate between liking a photo and posting short comments laced with emojis on other people's status updates. As she was scrolling, she noticed one of her friends had liked a local news story. *The caption read, Local Girl Starts Urban Community Farm on Campus.*

Jamie clicked on the link, and it brought her to a local news website. There was a picture of a young female college student standing among rows of leafy plants and vegetables in what looked to be an abandoned warehouse. Apparently, the young woman in the photo, Maya Collins, was enrolled in a master's degree program for urban development and was working on a project that dealt with finding a creative solution for abandoned warehouses and factories. She came up with an idea to turn the old buildings into urban greenhouses to grow community gardens for impoverished people. The seeds and produce would come from the donations of rural farmers, and the community gardens would be maintained by a group of volunteers. That way, any excess from the fall harvest wouldn't go to waste, and anyone who was willing to help maintain the community gardens could take a share of the proceeds. They could also donate their share to a less fortunate family.

Jamie didn't recognize the girl in the photo but was intrigued by the idea of the urban gardens. She had always wanted to start her own garden in the backyard but quickly became overwhelmed by the amount of work and dedication it would take. She would need to plot a special area with just the right amount of sun and shade, make sure the soil was rich enough, remember to use fertilizer every so often with the water, and find a way to keep critters from eating everything.

She could never decide on a finalized list of what to grow either. One day it would be strictly hearty tomatoes, but then half an hour on Pinterest would make her want to plant anything that would grow in North American soil. Jan had offered to help her get started, but gardening would never be his thing. In reality, the tiny plot of yard would probably just turn into a patch of weeds by the end of the summer anyway.

One of the logs on the fire gave a loud pop, breaking Jamie's concentration. She put her phone down and walked over to the glass door of the fireplace. The logs needed to be turned over, so she grabbed the onyx poker and jabbed the logs onto their bellies. Maybe the fire wouldn't last until Jan got back after all.

As she closed the glass door and put the poker back on the rack, she noticed movement from the front window. Allie's red coupe had just pulled up onto their newly paved street. She got out of the car wearing sunglasses and her outfit from last evening. It was probably good that Jamie had brewed a large pot of coffee.

Allie walked up the front steps and gave two rapid courtesy knocks as she walked right in the door. Jamie turned the music down on her phone and just smiled. "Rough morning?" she asked.

Allie gave a long dramatic sigh and said, "I left my goddamn tab open at the bar, so I had to drive over there and pick up my card. You were supposed to be the responsible one and remind me to close my tab! Now it looks like I was on a walk of shame."

Jamie just laughed and replied, "You went home alone last night, at least last I saw you. It's not my fault you wore the same outfit. And it's not like someone stole your identity. Maybe the bartender just wanted you to come back so he could see you again."

Allie pretended to be annoyed and said, "Please. That guy was a freaking tool. He wasn't even there this morning. And I need to do laundry. And these clothes were just sitting on the back of my chair, sooooo lay off!"

The two women walked toward the back of the house and into the kitchen. The coffee smelled like the beans had somehow caught on fire. Jamie hadn't even poured herself a cup yet. How long had Jan been in town?

Allie went straight to the cupboard and grabbed a white mug. She made a beeline toward the coffee pot and poured herself a cup. The pot sizzled and hissed when she placed it back on the burner. "So is Jan hiding out in the garage again, or what?" she asked as she took a loud sip.

Jamie grabbed herself a white mug and tentatively walked over to the coffee pot. She already regretted mentioning anything to Allie. "No, he went into town to grab some hangover munchies." She felt a pang of sudden guilt as soon as she finished the sentence. The ibuprofen was doing its job, but she still felt off this morning. "I mean, he just ran to get bagels, but he should be back anytime now."

"Hmmm," was all Allie had to add to the conversation. They both took a sip of their coffee and looked at the TV. Some suavely dressed salesman was standing in a car lot pitching an ad for an end of the year blowout sale. It sounded like he was yelling even though the volume of the TV was turned way down.

"So you wanna head to town later tonight and check out some of the festivities?" Jamie asked. She already knew Allie was planning on going. They had discussed it more than a few times last night.

"For sure," Allie replied. "I need to see when some of the other peeps are heading out, but we should plan on meeting up somewhere as a group. I heard there are going to be quite a few cops out too, so we should be smart about it."

Jamie nodded in agreement. She took another sip of the bitter liquid and noticed a slight twitch in her hand. She would need some food soon, or else the jitters would take over her whole body. She looked at her phone, but there were no messages from Jan. Maybe the line for bagels was out the door. Maybe the bakery was closed and he had to go somewhere else. Maybe he got a flat tire or something. Maybe she was just living inside her head too much and had to quit thinking about it.

Allie began talking about some random people that Jamie didn't know, but she pretended to listen anyway. She was glad for the distraction. Those paranoid stupid thoughts kept nagging her brain, and it was starting to irritate her. She was probably just getting herself worked up about nothing, but she still couldn't shake that weird feeling in the pit of her stomach. Today really was starting to suck.

CHAPTER FOUR

Sixty to one hundred beats per minute is the usual rate of a healthy human heart at rest. The doctor had always informed Gunner that he fell on the high end of that spectrum, but he was still healthy and unique. The doctor would put one end of the stethoscope in the young boy's ear, and they would both listen to the rhythmic succession of beats. Ba boom...Ba boom...Ba boom...Ba boom...Ba BA boom.... The doctor said it was something called extrasystole: an occasional extra heartbeat. It wasn't very common, but it wasn't anything that should be worrisome. Gunner used to think he was special.

Now, as he was carefully driving back to his house after such a bizarre morning, he could feel the palpitations in his throat. Every so often, the extra tick made him flinch just slightly. What the hell was going on? The surrounding scenery along the highway was just a coalescence of random shapes and muted color. Gunner needed some time to process all this information and recharge his batteries.

He didn't even remember much of the drive home before he almost missed the turn to his house. As the SUV took a sharp turn onto his usually vacant street, the distracted man had to swerve to keep from hitting a red coupe parked in front of the driveway entrance. He slammed on the brakes and cranked the steering wheel to the right in order to avoid barreling into the ditch. As the vehicle came to an abrupt stop, Gunner tensed his shoulders and unclenched his hands from the wheel. He whipped his head back and glared at the red car. "Fuckin Allison!" he yelled. *How much goddamn time do they need to spend together?* he thought. *It's not enough to be out drinking together, but they need to nurse each other's hangover too?* He could feel the extra palpitation in his forehead now.

The young man threw his vehicle in reverse and then pulled forward into the driveway and drove it back into the garage. He killed the engine and sat in the vehicle for a few minutes to collect himself. Maybe he could just creep in the back door, toss the food on the counter, and then lock himself in the bedroom upstairs. As he pondered his next move, Gunner took two deep breaths and massaged his aching temples. The smell of raspberries and bagels was starting to give him a nauseous feeling. Food always had a way of turning Gunner's stomach when he was over-tired or stressed.

He suddenly had a *deja vu* moment of sitting in the garage taking warm swigs from his old flask. A half-eaten raspberry toaster strudel had been lying on a plate next to the workbench. He briefly yearned for that fallacious sense of comfort when the whiskey would slide down his throat and make his head feel like he was floating underwater. The memory sent shudders down the back of his spine. He closed his eyes and shook his head. It's amazing how those poignant thoughts still lurk, submerged in a murky subconscious. Just when the antelope feels safe enough to take a drink at the riverbank, the crocodile pops up out of nowhere and shocks the hell out of the antelope. Hopefully, the antelope anticipates the attack before the inevitable happens. Gunner tried to remember how long it had been since he actually sat and shared at a meeting. *Not long enough*, he thought to himself. He didn't have the patience to deal with that level of narcism yet.

The reluctant man grabbed the food and wandered toward the back door of the house. Sleepiness began to tug at his eyelids as he dragged his feet the entire way. When he reached the door, he tried to slip inside as slowly and secretively as he could, but it was all for naught because the two ladies were sitting at the kitchen table.

"Jan's baaaaack!" yelled Allie. "What did you get for us?"

Gunner winced as the cacophonous sound waves rattled his poor eardrums. It was amazing how someone so little could produce that much noise, especially after a presumable night on the town. If Gunner had just been told he won ten million dollars and a new Ferrari, he would still need a shot of morphine and a frontal lobotomy to be able to stand Allie for more than five minutes. She KNEW he hated when she called him Jan, but she just liked to induce a reaction. *Little Miss Spotlight, Center Stage*, he thought.

"I picked up some bagels with raspberry something-or-other," he said, tossing the bag on the counter. "Knock yourselves out."

Jamie looked up from the TV and gave a loud sigh. "I thought I told you to get blueberry bagels," she whined. "You don't ever listen to me. They're not even the same color! You're always off in your own little world!"

Gunner turned to face her, visibly annoyed. "I just went into town to get some food as a favor to you, and you're gonna complain that it's not the right berry for the bagel? Raspberry, blueberry, who fuckin cares? Go get your own food if I don't do it right. Just eat something so you can cure yet another hangover."

Jamie grunted and turned toward the cupboards. "Whatever, I'll just have some cereal."

Allie decided to pipe in and exclaim, "Oooh! All for me then!" She eagerly grabbed the bag and tore it open. "They're all smashed together!" she yelled, still deciding to shovel them into her tiny mouth. She even chewed her food obnoxiously.

Gunner glanced at the TV to try to distract himself from Allie's crude eating behavior. There was a commercial for the six o'clock evening news that was going to feature the upcoming Harvest Moon Fall Festival, the dangers of texting and driving, and the search for a young local lady. The same picture from the park was briefly flashed on the screen before the commercial ended.

"That's crazy!" said Allie with a mouth full of bagels. "I heard that girl went for a jog like a week ago and never came back. She just literally ran away." Then Allie gave an inappropriate little giggle, probably because she thought she had said something clever.

Gunner decided he had had enough of people in general right now and needed to be alone. He immediately left the kitchen and made his way to the stairs. The young man waited until he got up to the bedroom before he took off his shoes and sweatshirt. There was no point in spending any more time downstairs if it wasn't absolutely necessary. He thought about taking a shower as he fell onto the bed. That idea faded quickly because sleep surreptitiously crawled over his skin and invaded his body.

* * *

The rain had been pounding the bay window for a while. A yellow car was parked, still running, in the driveway. A strange man sat in the driver's seat waiting with a bored look on his face. Jan sat nervously on the couch. There were cushions strewn all over the floor. A lamp had been knocked over, the shade bent. The picture on the mantle was turned on its side.

He could hear the low mumble of his father's even-keeled voice trying to creep through the wall. It was too inaudible to make out actual words. There was silence for a few seconds, then a loud sigh. The floorboards began to creak behind Jan. He turned his head to see his mother close the door behind her. He saw her through the bay window. She had a suitcase. She didn't seem to care about the rain. She climbed in the back of the yellow car, and it drove away.

Jan knew he had to sit on the couch or go to his room when Mommy was in her peaks and valleys. Fredrick was standing by the side of the couch. He tried to explain that Mommy was going to get help because she had been in too many valleys lately. Jan just sat and stared at the rain.

Gunner was chasing somebody, a female. He couldn't quite catch up to her. He couldn't see her face, but he knew it was his mother. They were running on the gravel road by his childhood house. He tried to yell, but no sound came. His legs felt like dead weight. Then, they were running in darkness. There were trees on both sides of the road. She kept pulling away.

Gunner tried to keep pace, but now he was falling over branches. He watched her disappear.

Gunner was leaning on his car door while he was driving, frantically trying to avoid hazards in the road. He cranked the wheel to the left and then hard to the right. His car door suddenly opened. He reached out to try to grab anything within reach. Everything seemed to be going in slow motion. He finally embraced the inevitable and let himself fall.

* * *

Gunner shot up in bed. He looked outside the bedroom window. Was it early morning or late afternoon? He looked at the clock on the nightstand—it read four-fifteen. It must be late afternoon. The disoriented man rubbed his eyes for a few seconds and then waited for them to adjust to the darkness of the room. He tried to calculate how long he had been out, but his brain was too fuzzy after just waking up from a hard crash.

Restful sleep was a luxury Gunner could rarely afford. The only time he ever slept during the day was when he was too exhausted to remain conscious. He always felt worse after a long afternoon nap than he did when he was struggling to keep his eyes open. It was like being in a state of sleep purgatory. He was too tired and muddled to concentrate on anything, but he couldn't go back to sleep because his sleep pattern was out of whack.

Today was no different. The dazed man shook his head to clear the fogginess from his brain, but it was no use. He decided to just throw the sheets off and climb out of bed. He fumbled around the nightstand, searching for his hoodie. When he couldn't find it, the young man got frustrated and slammed one of the drawers. He decided he was hungry and abruptly went downstairs to the kitchen.

Gunner was greeted by a note on the kitchen counter. It read, "Didn't want to wake you. Me and Allie went to Chinos. I grabbed your sweatshirt cuz Allie was cold. Don't wait up."

Well, that solved the mystery of the missing sweatshirt. If it ever came back, it would probably have an aroma of stale beer and cigarette smoke enmeshed in the fabric. The only way it was coming back was if they both decided to crash here tonight. "I liked that fuckin sweatshirt!" Gunner yelled at the note. He crumpled the piece of paper and threw it at a cupboard. *Well, I guess what's mine is both of theirs in this marriage*, the young man thought to himself.

He opened the cupboard and stared at the nearly barren shelves, seething for a few minutes. His mind began to play flashbacks of all the times Allie had "borrowed" something that belonged to him. Among the list of casualties were sweatshirts, laptop cords, phone chargers, movies, and a nice pair of leather gloves he had received for a birthday one year. He didn't even have the gloves long enough to become emotionally attached, but he never saw them again, and it really pissed him off now that he was thinking about them. Luckily, his grumbling stomach snapped him back to reality as he remembered why he came into the kitchen in the first place.

There wasn't much to eat on the shelves or in the fridge besides a few essentials. Gunner tried to think of a recipe that would allow him to use cheese, buffalo sauce, powdered sugar, milk, and spaghetti noodles and turn them into something remotely edible. After approximately ten seconds of concentration, he sat down at the kitchen table and booted up the laptop. If there was some kind of crazy concoction with those ingredients, the Internet would know.

As the computer slowly started to wake up from its long nap, the groggy man thought about what the wolf meat would taste like if it were slathered in buffalo sauce. It would probably result in the same sort of travesty as eating a rib-eye steak with ketchup. The true flavor of the meat would be drowned by the overpowering flavor of the sauce. Gunner quickly dismissed the notion as soon as he realized what he was thinking.

Once the computer was finished loading and updating, the curious man began to search for ways to prepare the wolf meat. He came across quite a variety of mixed reviews. People in this country just weren't accustomed to eating anything that resembled a dog. There were some helpful responses to people with similar inquiries, but there were also a lot of negative, condescending remarks. If everyone kept a cow as a pet and associated humanistic characteristics with it, Americans might have a harder time eating beef too.

There were quite a few posts that basically stated that wolf meat should be cooked and consumed at one's own risk. Wolves had been known to carry parasites and disease, but if the meat was harvested and prepared properly, it should be generally safe to eat. Gunner hadn't noticed any signs that the meat was tainted or that the animal had suffered from disease earlier that morning, so he just needed to be sure to prepare it properly. He already had a general idea of how he was going to prepare it. He just wanted to see if there were any special tricks or tips offered by people who had done it before.

After reading some more excerpts, Gunner concluded that the meat should be tenderized fairly well and cooked over high heat. That should keep the meat from getting too tough or dry. He was debating if he should fire up the grill. The young man also thought about what to cook with the meat. He definitely wanted to try a little bit without any seasoning, but he also wanted to be sure to make an edible meal. Some of the possibilities would be to mix it into a stew, cook it with vegetables and marinate it, or mix the meat in a tortilla and add cilantro and salsa.

Whichever way he finally decided to prepare the meal, he absolutely needed to go to the store and pick up some additional ingredients. The scarce amount of food that happened to be in the kitchen wasn't what he needed for this type of meal. Gunner closed the laptop, quickly scribbled a list of ingredients on a Post-it note, grabbed his keys, and went to the SUV.

The sun had disappeared for the evening, and the cool night air left a sharp bite. As Gunner opened the car door, he paused for a moment to try and remember what he'd left in the back of the SUV. He curiously scratched his head as if the fogginess would evaporate from his brain. The hunter decided to open the back door and check just to be safe.

All that was in the back of the vehicle was a blanket, an old tarp, and a few miscellaneous tools. None of it was evidence to incriminate him in any sort of crime, nor was it considered any type of hazard to be carrying while driving. Gunner breathed a slight sigh of relief and quickly shut the back door. It was time to run to town and do some grocery shopping.

* * *

Jamie sat at a small table inside of Chino's and lazily sipped her spiked apple cider. It was happy hour, and they were promoting a two-for-one hard cider special for the festival, so the place was crammed with an eclectic mix of people. She was waiting for Allie to finish ordering drinks they didn't need from the hot bartender way down at the other end of the restaurant bar. He seemed way too busy to even notice her tiny frame, but that just made her embrace the challenge by practically sitting on top of the bar.

Jamie was still incensed over the last interaction she had had with Jan. He didn't need to be so scathing toward her. He was the one that volunteered to get food but just came back with a random bag of assorted items and basically threw it at her. It had felt like a backhanded compliment, and it still stung. He might as well have just said she was pretty, even for someone pushing thirty.

Even if Jamie had wanted him to come out tonight, he probably would have fabricated some bullshit excuse to stay home…or wherever he had been this morning and a few nights earlier this week. When he actually was home, it seemed like he either had his face buried in the computer screen or he was holed up somewhere cleaning his hunting gear. Every time she asked him what he was up to, he just dismissed her by saying, "Just sorting some things out, don't worry about it." He was becoming that irritable, closed off shell of a man he had been when his drinking had become the worst; after his father died.

It had taken some time to get used to the new Jan who didn't drink, but he seemed genuinely happier without it. His mood swings were calmer, and he seemed to have more peace of mind these days. He had never been violent toward anyone who didn't deserve it when he was drinking, but he usually turned all of his anger and resentment inward when he used to get upset. When the situation would get to a boiling point, Jamie would have to leave him alone until he sobered up. It was like trying to diffuse a ticking time bomb while wearing a blindfold.

After Jan got sober for good, he used to come out during the Harvest Moon Festival and just order sodas or plain apple cider. He at least made an effort to be part of the conversation, even though Jamie knew he would much rather be hunting by himself. He needed to be around people, especially because this time of year was so hard on him. But now, he wouldn't even come out at all.

Now he just disappeared for brief stretches of time and came back like he had gone to fill up on gas or something. Maybe he was sneaking out to meetings and unloading his thoughts on anonymous strangers. Maybe he felt guilty for having to do it that way and didn't want to address the elephant in the room. Maybe he actually went to visit his father's grave for the first time since the funeral. Or maybe he needed to deal with his problems the only way he knew how.

Jamie slammed the last of the harsh rum and cinnamon kick to her taste buds just as Allie showed up with more drinks. She gracefully twisted her tiny body between the amoebic clusters of people without spilling.

"Brought us round two, minus the barkeep's significant other status. I found out his last name, though, so I can Facebook stalk him to see if he's dating anyone," she said with a devilish smile.

Jamie laughed and said, "Was it worth getting scolded by the bouncer to 'kindly get the fuck off the bar'?"

"It got his attention, didn't it?" she shot back.

"Glad you were willing to sacrifice a little dignity," Jamie said as she reached for the spiked cider. "So, what's the plan for the rest of the night?"

"Well, it sounds like one of Remmy's friends from high school is throwing a huge bonfire party out in the sticks. I say we go crash that. It sounds like the place is big enough, so if we need to sleep it off there, we could."

"Remmy?" Jamie asked, at a loss.

"You know, tall guy, perfect fade haircut, nicely trimmed beard, smooth dark skin."

"You mean the guy from the call center of the clinic?" Jamie asked. "Isn't his last name like Remmick or something, but he usually likes to be called Deuce? I'll bet you don't even know his real name, but you're already calling him Remmy."

"He's a cool guy! I talk with him when we go on our smoke breaks. I'm sure Deuce isn't his real name either, but I like the way Remmy sounds better. When he's on his way in from a smoke break, he's always casually flicking his cigarette and saying in his deep sultry voice, 'You ladies ever wanna kick it, just hit me up,'" Allie said in her mock manly voice. "I say we take him up on his offer."

Jamie took a tentative sip of her drink. Allie had driven them here, but she planned on leaving her car overnight. Whatever Jamie decided to do, she would have to catch a ride from somebody. She didn't necessarily want to go home early, especially if it meant she would have to risk interrupting whatever Jan was doing.

"I think I've shared like five sentences with anyone from the call center," Jamie admitted. "Do you know if anyone else we know is going to be at this party?" She was already dreading that this was going to turn into one of those post-high school bashes where people tried desperately to relive their glory days.

"Well, the two techs from last night said they had planned to meet us here, but they got delayed. I'm pretty sure they will go. I'll message some more people and see if we can at least get somebody to give us a ride."

Allie went to work texting and messaging her contacts from various social media. Jamie took another long sip on her drink and looked at her blank phone screen. The screensaver was a picture of a beautiful sunset taken from a beach in California. For a minute, she remembered the way the Pacific breeze had sifted through her hair when she had snapped the photo. The taste of salt on her lips and the caress of sand between her toes had been so satisfying. It had been the perfect end to a perfect day. The memory brought a smile to her face until someone from the packed restaurant rudely bumped into her chair.

The inebriated asshole didn't even apologize before pushing through the sea of people. Jamie just rolled her eyes and looked around at the animated faces that surrounded her. Even though she couldn't move her chair more than six inches without bumping into somebody else, she still felt like she was sitting alone on the couch at home.

CHAPTER FIVE

Yellow dots of flickering light quivered through the darkness. They could be seen dancing near the road and playfully hiding within the woods. It was customary for a lot of people to celebrate the Harvest Moon Festival by lighting bonfires on the second Saturday of October. If you lived outside of the city, there was a good chance that you or at least one of your neighbors was going to construct a blaze that could be seen from the highway. It was easier to see the cloistered fires being lit from the confines of the trees now that the fields had been mostly devoured by hungry machinery. There was almost an unofficial competition to see whose fire could be seen from the furthest distance away.

Gunner had only participated for one year. Not only was his blaze worthy of a sacrifice to the gods, but he passed out drunk before putting out the fire at the end of the night and almost burned the house down. Jamie made sure they never hosted another bonfire party again.

Even though that one year ended up being reckless, Gunner had always liked sitting around a bonfire. There was just something about falling into a mesmerizing trance while watching the flames swirl and hearing the wood pop that made him feel at ease. He would still consider attending the gatherings if these parties hadn't become just another excuse for people to get obnoxiously intoxicated and cause unnecessary drama. The young man didn't need a bunch of drunken acquaintances to be present in order to revel in the ambiance of a fire. In fact, he thought about primitively cooking the meat over an open flame down by the slaughterhouse in his backyard. He was almost positive that Jamie and Allie would be bouncing around to the bonfire parties anyway, so there wouldn't be any interruptions.

Slowly but surely, the yellow lights that scattered across the sides of the highway began to dissipate as the vehicle approached the city. It was illegal to have an open fire in your yard if you lived within the city limits. Some of the local restaurants found a loophole in the law and tried to lure potential customers by having a propane "fire pit" on an outdoor patio with discounted appetizers and drinks, but most people would agree that it just wasn't the same as feeding an open blaze that tried so vigorously to touch the sky. Extra law enforcement was also on patrol for additional public safety, but that didn't deter very many people from having a good time.

Even though a lot of city-dwellers eventually made their way to the bonfires, the streets were still fairly busy this early in the evening. There seemed to be a small convoy of cars at every stoplight. Groups of people came out of the quaint stores along the main drag and meandered on both sides of the street. Some of them even darted in between traffic, causing Gunner to become slightly agitated. "Get the fuck out of the way!" he mumbled under his breath as he tapped the steering wheel with his fingers. His mind was still hazy from the long crash earlier in the day, so inconsiderate people jumping in front of his two-thousand-pound vehicle probably wasn't in their best interest.

It was taking way too long to get to the store from this route, so the impatient young man edged the SUV near the end of the sidewalk and took an abrupt right turn at the light. He decided it would be faster to get what he needed at the mega shopping center on the edge of the city. It always seemed to be packed no matter what time of day, but most places were probably crawling with eager hordes right now. Gunner could just sift his way through the crowd, use the self-checkout, and be winnowed back to his house in no time, at least in theory.

After a few rolling stops and speed limit infractions, Gunner made his way to the zoo that happened to be the parking lot. A colossal, newly constructed white tent sat in the middle. It had an eerie soft glow resonating from the inside that made it appear as though it were hosting some sort of circus attraction. The outside was littered with shapely pumpkins that hunkered against the crevice of where the tent tried to touch the black pavement. Some were meticulously carved into patterns of wheat fields and various antique farm tilling tools. They were supposed to resemble and depict old folk stories of harvest reaping, but most were just picked from the ground and available to be sold to the masses. A few stray hay bales were hastily tossed around the pavement too.

Inside the tent was a maze of tables that held arts and crafts made by local artists. Some of the young pop culture artists tried to cash in on Halloween, but most of the art was designed in the true nature of the Harvest

Moon Festival. Each piece told its own story.

Gunner parked toward the end of the parking lot and slowly walked to the entrance of the tent. He could smell freshly brewed apple cider and cinnamon drifting from somewhere nearby. The wind tossed some stray pieces of golden hay onto his pants, so he brushed it off with his hand. The young man kept one of the dry, rough straws and twirled it between his fingers. He always liked to snap it in increments of four equal pieces. He then rubbed them together and let the pieces disintegrate back into the wind. It was an odd habit that had stuck with him since he was a boy.

When he approached the opening of the tent, quite a few interesting art pieces caught his eye. One of the first tables featured a good-sized wood carving that was hollowed to different thicknesses and smoothed over with fastidious detail. The table next to it was layered with abstract colors that were sprayed upon different textured canvases. They all formed a collage that seemed to follow a theme. One of the tables in the middle of the tent had a crude looking sculpture that had thin black pieces of twisted metal jutting from tin cylinders. As he scoured the tent, he noticed that most of the weary-faced artists were engaged with enthusiastic passersby. The young man would have loved to sit one-on-one with some of the artists and listen to the story behind his or her artwork, but that wasn't going to be a realistic possibility tonight. Gunner could feel the energy being sucked out of the tent like an air mattress being deflated. He decided he might swing by tomorrow while the rest of the city succumbed to sleep. There would probably be less of a chance of feeling like a clown was going to jump out from behind a table and murder him if he entered the tent during daylight anyway.

As he began briskly making his way to the store entrance, he felt a strong jolt to the side of his leg. The curious man reached into his pocket and pulled out his phone. Jamie had sent him a text message.

So whats been goin on l8ly...like last few nights??

Amazing what a little liquid courage will do. Gunner just stared at his phone for a few seconds, letting the reality of the situation sink in. He was considering if he really wanted to fester this storm just yet.

* * *

Jamie laid her pool cue against the side of the green table and walked over to the bar where her mom and some of her friends were sitting. They had been chatting incessantly in good humor all evening. Everyone was getting together to catch up and retell old stories over the holidays. It was getting late, and the bar was starting to thin out, but people were still having a good time.

Gunner wobbled over to what he thought was a good angle for his next shot at the #3 ball. This was the first Christmas he and Jamie were spending together as a couple. They had met a bunch of Jamie's friends for drinks earlier in the evening, but now it was just the two of them and some guy from Jamie's high school playing a cutthroat game of pool.

Gunner had met Jamie's mom and stepdad a few times before tonight. He didn't know them well, but he knew he did not like Rob the first time they were introduced. He adored Evelyn and could see a lot of similar traits in Jamie, but Rob had rubbed him the wrong way since day one.

Jamie's father died in a car crash when she was twelve. Not only was it sudden and unexpected, but Evelyn had only been working part time as a freelance artist designing brochures and other small print materials. She couldn't support two kids and herself on her menial salary. She had met Rob about a year after Jamie's father had passed, and they married three months later.

Rob was spending this evening entertaining some big shot clients for his company at a different location, which everyone seemed to think was perfectly fine. Jamie had mentioned that he tended to be gruff when he was drinking anyway. He surely would have gotten bored sitting around listening to Evelyn and her friends talk about arts and crafts, or whatever it was he assumed they discussed. And Jamie seemed to be enjoying the fact that her mom was having a fun girls' night out.

The mother and daughter chatted and laughed for a few minutes while the bartender poured some drinks. Gunner leaned over the green felt and tried to keep his balance while he took his next shot. He grazed the side of the cue ball and sent it spinning into the side pocket. "Well, fuck me!" he said, trying to sound pissed.

The other guy just laughed and went to grab the cue ball out of the pocket. "Whish colors am I again?" he slurred.

"Who fuckin cares?" Gunner chimed in. "Just show me a sick shot. I'll give you ten dollars if you can bank the blue one in the corner pocket."

The other guy chuckled again and yelled, "Deal!

Now put yo money on da table."

The two of them began taking turns smashing the balls on the table, trying to do "trick" shots. They tried to keep tabs on who sunk the most, but neither could agree on how much each sloppy shot was worth. This went on for a bit until the other guy decided he needed a smoke break. "Hold on, need a smokey treat," he said as he threw his coat on and stumbled out the backdoor.

There was only one ball left on the table, so Gunner tried to hit the cue ball around it. As he was lining up his next shot, Jamie came and stood silently next to him. She was obviously distraught about something. Gunner looked at her and then over at Evelyn. Her friends were leaving as a heavily intoxicated Rob was leaning next to the table. Evelyn's body was hunched forward as she stared at the table.

"Apparently, the meeting didn't go well with the big shots," Jamie said solemnly. Gunner sat on the pool table and tried to register what had just happened. Just a minute ago, everyone had been in good spirits, and the night was going well. Now Jamie just stood there frozen, her upper lip quivering ever so slightly. He really didn't know what to say.

Then he heard an almost inaudible gasp escape Jamie's lips when out of the corner of his eye, he saw Rob try to grab Evelyn's arm. Jamie was paralyzed. The look on her face was the same look a deer has after being shot and about to take its last breath.

Gunner made the decision right then and there that he never wanted to see that look on her face again. His heart began to race as he gritted his teeth and impulsively walked over to Evelyn's table. In those brief seconds, Rob had gotten more aggressive and was spitting something nasty to his wife while trying to get her to stand. Nobody else in the bar seemed to notice what was going on between the two. The only thing they noticed was when Gunner broke the pool cue over Rob's face. Officer Stansby had been the first one on the scene.

* * *

Six messages had been typed and deleted in response to Jamie's message before Gunner finally replied simply, *We'll talk when it's just you and I.* He didn't want to turn this into a two against one battle. He never won those battles, and they were starting to become more frequent. He just didn't want to deal with it right now, so he dumped his phone in his pocket and proceeded into the chaos of the store.

He began absentmindedly searching his coat pocket for the list he had scrawled on a Post-it note before he left. When he couldn't find it, he began wandering aimlessly through the store while flipping his coat inside out. He remembered putting it in his pocket. He just didn't know which one. After a fervent search, he finally found it in the left inside pocket where he used to keep his flask. As he uncrumpled the note, an unwelcome familiar smell of fermented yeast and subtle fruit invaded his nose. The highly alert man didn't need to look at the sign to know he was standing in aisle nineteen next to the whiskey, beer, and wine.

Gunner decided the riverbank wasn't safe, so he crumpled the note in his hand and didn't look down until he was at the opposite end of the store. He went down the last aisle and stood in the back corner facing a shelf that featured pain relievers and toothpaste. He closed his eyes and let the imperceptible noise around him flutter through his eardrums. "Just get what you need and leave," he whispered to himself. The problem with the mega shopping center was that it had everything.

The agitated man uncrumpled the blue paper in his hand and looked at the list. He realized that everything he needed was down three adjacent aisles. Gunner spent the next five minutes weaving and dodging around other shoppers and carried an armful of items to the self-checkout counter. All of the items were hastily dumped onto the counter and absentmindedly scanned. The robotic cashier voice couldn't even finish the instructions before the buttons had been pushed on the screen. Gunner threw everything into one plastic bag, darted for the sliding glass doors, and left the receipt spinning on the register. Once the whoosh of the doors opened and Gunner felt the gentle slap of dry air touch his face, he felt a sense of relief. It felt refreshing to be out of there. He looked up at the vast open sky, but all he could see was an ocean of black because the stars were drowned by the artificial light pollution in the parking lot. His surroundings were a terrible substitute for a bonfire beneath the stars and spotlight of pale moonlight.

The young man brought his attention to the parking lot and realized the exit was on the opposite side of where he parked. As he began walking in the direction of his vehicle, he heard some sort of singing or chanting coming from a group of people that had gathered in front of the circus tent. There must have been forty to fifty people dressed in similar robed costumes wearing an assortment of brightly colored masks. It was also customary for some people to wander the streets in costume and chant rhymes or play-act during the second weekend of October. As Gunner got closer to the group, he heard what they were chanting in unison.

"Tonight, we dance
We sing at last
Come out from silhouette"

It was an old chant that was supposed to lure the souls of the departed from the shadows. The apparitions were supposed to be able to blend in with the people who wore masks and walk among the living. For one night, the two vastly different worlds would become one. The people who wore masks were eventually supposed to help the departed souls find their way home and discover peace. A group of people always acted this scene at some point during the Harvest Moon Festival.

The chanting continued while the group of robed figures huddled together in the middle of the lot. Even though the masks were somewhat different, it was difficult to distinguish one person from the next. They all became one pulsating amoeba, constantly shifting and changing color.

Their footsteps marched to the beat of the chant that began to grow quieter. The robed figures kept repeating the same three lines until the audience had to strain to hear the voices. The chant became a whisper that gently lifted onto the breeze. It was as if the group feared their voices would cause the remaining leaves to fall from the tree branches.

As more and more people came out from the art tent and gathered around from the store and street, the chanting became louder and boisterous. This went on for a few minutes before, to the delight of the gathered crowd, people dressed like ghosts came wandering from their hiding places. The people dressed as ghosts joined the group of masked individuals, and they all started dancing around in a circle.

Gunner decided it was still entertaining to watch even though he had seen this act so many times before. He looked around at the crowd of onlookers and observed the merriment on most of their faces. Everybody seemed to be caught up in the festivity and soon began cheering and clapping. It was always fun because these acts were never scheduled and always spontaneous.

Almost everyone near Gunner had their phone pointed above the person in front of them, trying to record the impromptu show taking place in the center of the parking lot. Some people were even trying to take pictures of themselves with the actors dancing around in a circle behind them. It wasn't long before the crowd began to part as the actors sang and mingled with the audience. Most of the audience was overly eager to join the performance. Soon the whole parking lot was filled with people laughing, singing, and dancing.

Just when Gunner started to forget about how agitated he had just felt, and his shoulders started to relax, he felt something pelt the side of his face. He looked down to see what the culprit was and noticed a crumpled piece of paper next to his boot. The curious man reached down, opened it, and tried to read it in the light from the store window. It simply read, "I saw you in the woods last night."

The startled man spun around and saw the backs of a bunch of people in robes whirl past him. "What the fuck?" he yelled. Nobody could hear him over the singing of the actors or the cheering of the crowd. Somebody must have tossed it at him as they danced past him. He madly looked around, trying to search for a possible suspect, but it was no use. Whoever threw it had carefully blended back into the group.

* * *

Jamie shivered as she waited on the gravel road for Allie to finish talking to someone on her phone. It sounded like she was trying, as best she could, to drunkenly give directions. They had decided to just call a cab since it was surge pricing for all the ride share apps. It was basically the same price as a Lyft, but less of a wait to be picked up from Chinos.

The cab had dropped them off at an old farmhouse about twenty miles outside of the city. The driver nearly got lost, zigzagging down the unmarked rural roads and even had to pull over to make sure his GPS wasn't leading him into a plowed field or unmarked ditch. The poor guy didn't say much during most of the ride, but he became very agitated by the time they reached their destination. Hopefully, Allie had a better sense of where they were.

Jamie swaggered back and forth when she turned around to look at the massive bonfire that was taunting them at the end of the road. The flames looked like they were desperately trying to leap over the trees to come and grab her, but they couldn't quite reach. It almost looked like two separate fires had swirled together, or maybe the alcohol from her last drink was really starting to flow straight to her head.

She had finished her drink faster than she would have liked, but she had been more than happy to leave the bar when they did. Two guys with deep bloodshot eyes sat down at a table near them and barely spoke inside the noisy restaurant. They had just sat there and stared, almost leered, at Jamie and Allie. Jamie had felt their stares long before Allie had noticed either of them. They both had chewed fingernails and knuckles that looked like they had been in a bare-fisted boxing match recently. There was just something offsetting about the way their eyes didn't quite meet her gaze like they were looking through her or didn't quite see her.

She sometimes saw people like that come into the clinic. They always wore long-sleeved shirts to cover the marks on their arms, even during the dog days of July. When they were finally coerced to roll up their sleeves in order to draw blood, it was damn near impossible to find a usable vein. She would often get the same leering stares from those types of patients, and they were the reason she never left the clinic alone, especially at night.

Jan used to come and pick her up after her night shifts when they were first married because she would tell him about those types of patients. They were still in the honeymoon phase, and he wanted to be her knight in shining armor by making sure she came home safely, but sometimes his drinking started shortly after his own shift ended. When she awkwardly had to ask the security guard on duty to walk her to her car on a weekly basis, Jamie just made arrangements to always be scheduled with Allie.

"I'll just drop a pin, so make sure your phone is charged," Allie said as she hung up and walked over to Jamie. "Jeez, I didn't think it would be this difficult to find the place," she said while vigorously swiping her fingers on her screen. "That cab driver really fucked with my sense of direction."

Jamie just scoffed and replied, "Are you sure it's not just you?"

Allie ignored her but kept tapping on her phone screen. The two women began to walk down the gravel road toward the music, laughter, and black billowy smoke. It was as if the flames had started consuming a rubber tire or something. Jamie looked around at the barren fields and up at the white dots that speckled the clear night sky. She felt like she was back in high school heading to a kegger in the middle of nowhere. A nasty case of *deja vu* was settling in her stomach.

"Let's go grab a beer and find Remmy," Allie said as she put her phone in her back pocket. "He said they had a few coolers near the barn. I'm sure they'll let us snatch a few if we give them our best pouty faces."

"Let's stand by the fire for a bit," Jamie countered. "I need to warm myself up if I'm gonna be hanging out at an old school party in the woods," she said as she nearly tripped over her own feet.

"Yeah, I could use a little warmth," Allie agreed as they walked up to the blaze at the edge of the driveway to the old farmhouse. It felt like a furnace was set to full blast and aimed directly at their faces. There was a group of six people standing at least five feet away from a pile of burning logs, pallets, broken furniture, and what looked like the remnants of a small black bike tire.

"Welcome, ladies," one of the guys standing near the edge of the fire said. "Sorry about the smell. Someone thought it would be HILARIOUS to throw a rubber tire onto the pile," he said, staring at his friend.

Jamie didn't know any of the men or women standing in the tight-knit circle. They all looked like they belonged to the same high school clique, minus the letterman's jackets and rampant outbreaks of acne. She wondered which two had been the homecoming king and queen.

"Hey, do any of you know Dion Remmick?" Allie asked while turning her palms toward the fire.

"Deuce? Yeah, he's over by the barn, last I saw him," the guy who supposedly threw the tire on the fire said. "He might be a little preoccupied at the moment, though," he said, tapping his nose.

"Luke!" one of the girls scolded, shaking her head.

The guy's face turned red, and he tried to force a laugh. "He's probably got a cold or something," he said, trying to play it off as a joke.

Allie laughed along and said, "No, it's fine, we're just here to have a good time too."

"See," Luke said to the girl in his clique. "Don't be so dramatic. We're all adults here." He turned to Allie and asked, "So how do you know Deuce?"

"We actually work with him at the clinic," Allie responded to the chagrin of the group. "Don't worry, we're not narks or anything. We got halfway to fucked up at Chinos before heading over here, so no judgment."

This seemed to ease their apprehension a little. Jamie reached for her phone and checked the screen, but there were no new messages. Somehow, she wasn't surprised. She knew it was childish to risk starting a fight through text, but it seemed to be the only way to get a reaction lately.

"Heads up, we got more shit to burn!" some guy yelled as he and two of his friends walked over with some pallets and miscellaneous wood scraps. Everyone around the fire took a few tentative steps back while the three guys tossed some more fuel into the hell pit. Everyone except Jamie cheered when the sparks exploded into the air and the fire raged into the night sky.

Yep, just like high school, Jamie thought to herself.

She looked at the old farmhouse and cringed. It had to have been worse than anywhere she had ever crashed in college. It looked like a place someone might go to score some heroin or cook some meth. It probably smelled like rot and mildew in the basement, if it even had one. Maybe it was just a bomb shelter underneath the house. If that was the case, the mice must have taken up residence too.

Jamie leaned over and whispered to Allie, "Are you sure you wanna hang here for the rest of the night? That house looks pretty sketch."

Allie glanced at it and replied, "Let's go see about grabbing a beer from the cooler. Who knows," she said while pointing at her nose. "Maybe we can find something entertaining to do in the barn. Plus, Braden, Val, and Desi are on their way, so we gotta at least wait for them."

As the two ladies started to walk away from the bonfire, someone shouted, "Oh shit, hide the drugs!" The high school clique stopped what they were doing and looked around the yard.

"Too late, you're all busted," came a reply from the gravel road. Everyone looked in that direction and then relaxed when they noticed who it was.

"Mare, good to see you!" one of the women shouted. "You actually come to party?"

"No, I'm on duty later tonight, unfortunately," she said as she walked up and stood near the fire. Her mocha hair was pulled back into a tight ponytail, and she was wearing a light brown lamb skin leather jacket with jeans over her freshly polished black boots. She couldn't have been older than thirty, but she looked like she was trying to pass for early twenties. Maybe she was going undercover to bust underage drinking parties. "Looks like you guys have quite the rager going here tonight," she said casually.

"Oh, we're just getting started," the guy named Luke said. "You think you could leave us some party favors for later? I know we could find some interesting things to do with a taser. Or maybe you could 'lose' some weed you confiscated off some little punk."

"I should taze whoever threw that tire in the flames," she said as she waved black smoke away from her face.

The others just yelled, "Ohhhhhh!" as they pushed a red-faced Luke toward her. "Let it rip!" one of the ladies yelled.

"I would love to, but I actually just wanted to pop in to say hi, and also remind you idiots that Stansby is looking for ANY reason to pull people over tonight. Be cool about catching a sober ride. Plus, I don't want to stay too long. Otherwise, I feel like I'll become an accomplice to your shenanigans."

"Remember when she used to be cool?" one of the guys joked.

The group laughed just as another group of people Jamie didn't know walked up from the gravel road. Jamie gave a weird glance toward Allie as an array of hugs and fist-bumps erupted between both groups. She felt like the band geeks who had stumbled upon the jock and cheerleader party after a football game. Nobody seemed to even notice they were standing there.

As the two began to pull away from the bonfire and head toward the barn again, Mary edged her way over and pleasantly said, "Hey ladies, how's your night going so far?"

"Pretty good," Jamie replied with furrowed eyebrows. "We just showed up a few minutes before you and were on our way to grab a beer," she said, pointing toward the barn.

"Oh, okay, I don't mean to bother you. I'm just making sure people are being smart tonight. I used to go to these parties and bounce around from place to place when I was younger, and I know how easily they can get out of hand in a hurry," she said, looking at Jamie. "I'm not trying to preach or anything. I just want to be sure everyone is safe and has a sober ride."

Jamie felt like she was silently being accused of something. "Yeah, I can call a cab or my husband, Jan, to come pick us up later. We didn't even drive here anyway, so worst case scenario is we end up walking."

"Oh, is Jan at a different party?" she asked as if they were old friends catching up over lunch.

"No, he'd rather be alone stalking animals in the woods," Allie chimed in.

"Avid hunter, I take it," Mary replied. "He must be chomping at the bit getting ready for deer season. It's gotta be hard knowing there is such an overpopulation this year. Has he been out scouting some areas around here, or does he have a place he usually likes to go?"

"I don't know. You'd have to ask him," Jamie replied more dismissively than she had meant. "I mean, hunting was never really my thing, and he hasn't been home much lately, so that's probably a fair assumption. I guess it comes with the territory during the fall season when you're married to a hunter."

Mary's eyes gave a contemplative stare into the woods beyond the old farmhouse. "I know what you mean. My father was usually MIA when the calendar turned to October. He said he never liked to hunt the same area twice, so he would hop in his truck and disappear for hours on end. When he finally came back, and we'd ask him where he'd been, he said he had been roaming around looking for a prime new place to set up his deer stand. At least that's what he always told my mother," she said with the faintest hint of a snide smirk. "Does your husband usually stay in the area, or does he disappear on the weekends?"

"Like I said, you'd have to ask him," Jamie said.

Mary just smiled and said, "Okay, sorry to bother you ladies. Be safe tonight and find a sober ride." She turned around and walked back toward the orange blaze.

Jamie and Allie continued walking toward the barn. "What the fuck was that about?" Allie whispered.

"I don't know," was all Jamie could respond. The sinking pit in her stomach was festering into a cavern. She hated herself for subconsciously falling back into old habits of her own. Why did she feel the need to make excuses for Jan? There was no crime in preparing for fall hunting season. He was always off at a moment's notice when the opportunity to give chase to wild game presented itself. It was an innate itch ingrained within a perpetual cycle that shifted with the seasons. This season was no different. He had just never completely come back from the last cycle.

Jamie always dreaded the long cold nights alone on the couch at home, but she was able to grit her teeth and bear it knowing they wouldn't last forever. She knew the season would end, and the house wouldn't feel so empty eventually, but this season felt like winter was coming sooner than expected. The best cure for the winter blues was sunshine and a smooth sandy beach. "Let's go find that cooler," she said.

CHAPTER SIX

Frederick used to spend the long winter months crafting and molding unique hunting bows. He would disappear for hours while he wielded his knife with exacting strokes against robust pieces of wood. Each design produced a highly functional tool blended with an aesthetic elegance.

Once Frederick became quite skilled in his craft, he decided to make one for Jan. The boy had just turned ten and was becoming an avid pupil while he tagged along on his father's hunts. The two had never been bow hunting together yet, so Fredrick thought it would be a good time to start teaching. The only problem was that all of Fredrick's bows were too big for his son, so he decided to make a smaller one that winter.

The bow was made from hickory wood because it was easy to find and forgiving of knots. The final design of the bow looked thin and flimsy at first glance, but the arch and bend of the wood was carved and narrowed with precision. The top and bottom portions of the bow were also carved into spirally circles, portraying the bow and stern of a Viking warship. When the design was complete, the only thing left to do was string it.

Frederick had his son come down to the basement

and string it himself. If Jan was going to have a weapon, he ought to know how to operate and take care of it. Jan had made the loops and attached the string to the lower tip of the bow just like his father showed him. The part that gave him fits was trying to hold the bow between his legs and carefully bend the top so he could loop the string. The string needed to be shorter than the length from top to bottom, and the bow needed to be bent in order to create enough tension to be able to propel an arrow. Jan kept trying and trying with no success, and his father wouldn't help him.

As Gunner sped away from the parking lot of the shopping center, he found himself replaying that memory of trying to string his first bow. He remembered having tears of frustration, being so irritable that he felt like pulling his hair out. He would have smashed and destroyed that bow if his father hadn't taken it away from him and walked upstairs.

When the bow was given back to him, he tried a few more times and was finally able to string it properly. Again he had received no help from Frederick. All the anger Jan felt toward Frederick instantly vanished once he placed his raw fingers against the taut string and gently plucked it. There was so much tension in the string that it made a high-pitched ping sound when it was released from the boy's fingers.

The SUV swerved into the opposite lane and quickly veered back as Gunner tried to read the address on his phone. The edges of the screen began to turn a bluish green before he realized how tightly his fist was clamped around it. The voicemail he had left for Jamie had resulted in a text of the bonfire party address they were currently attending. He generally knew where the place was but was almost positive he had never been there before tonight. Gunner glanced from his phone to the rearview mirror and then to the road in front of him. He gave half a thought to plugging the address into the GPS on his phone but decided to concentrate on the road.

The last thing the young man wanted to do was deal with a bunch of obnoxious drunks, but maybe it would be easier to navigate the conversation and sway around sensitive information without drawing too much attention to himself. People were in a celebratory mood and most likely highly inebriated. Not too many people would be inclined to give two shits about the sober guy at the party.

As Gunner turned off the highway and onto a gravel road, he could see that this party would be in the running for the most visible blaze. Orange light danced on the treetops and beckoned any nearby presence to come closer. A caravan of vehicles was neatly lined along the side of the road, sitting silently beneath the massive trees. Gunner parked in the back of the line and began the quarter-mile trek to the celebration.

He could hear muffled voices, high pitched laughter, and the hum of a music beat as he crept closer. The young man ventured around a car and into the edge of the woods. He investigated his surroundings and checked behind him. His vehicle was still last in line, and nobody else was on the road. He waited in the shadows for a few minutes and let his eyes fully adjust to the darkness.

Gunner could still see the scrawled letters on the

piece of paper in his head. I saw you in the woods last night. He obviously hadn't recognized the handwriting at all. Every time it replayed in his head, a creepy overwhelming sense of dread overcame the young hunter and made him feel as though someone was watching him. The skin and hair on his arms raised, and a slow chill slid down his back. He waited in the comforting shelter of the thicket for a good ten minutes, digging his fingernails into his palms until he was sure nobody had followed him here. Maybe it was just a sick prank because anybody who knew him could probably guess that he had been hunting, especially this time of year. The only question was, who had the motive?

Gunner finally decided he had spent enough time in the thicket and decided to venture the rest of the way to the party. He walked into the clearing at the end of the gravel driveway and looked around for Jamie. An acrid billow of black smoke blew in his direction and stung his eyes for a few seconds. He coughed and waited for the smoke to dissipate before resuming a brief scan of the farmhouse property. The anxious man only noticed a handful of mutual acquaintances he had met through Jamie or Allie at some point over the years. In fact, he didn't even remember half of their names, but he almost never forgot a face. He made a brief nod to a small cluster of people and walked around the massive pile of burning branches.

Gunner carefully careened around a bunch of wobbly groups of people and made his way across the lawn toward the barn. He spotted Jamie standing next to Allie, surrounded by four unfamiliar guys. He hesitated for a brief second, half-expecting them to shoot a suspicious look his way and start laughing about the practical joke they had just played on him. After the ridiculous thought passed, the observant young man noticed that it might take a bit of a scene to get any attention thrown his way.

Nobody noticed Gunner until he walked up behind Jamie and visibly tapped his hand on her shoulder. She turned her head and said, "Hey."

Allie turned her attention toward them and added, "Oh look, Jan decided to make a special appearance!" The other guys chuckled and took swigs from their drinks.

"Glad I could brighten your day, Allie," Gunner retorted. He then looked at Jamie and quietly mumbled, "Can we talk?"

The two of them walked out of earshot from the others. Jamie just stood with her arms crossed, waiting for him to speak.

"So, what was that text about?" he asked.

She replied, "I don't know. With everything that's been going on lately, I don't know what to think sometimes. I really don't wanna do this here and now."

He just kind of stared at her, not knowing how to proceed. Even if he told her the truth, she probably wouldn't believe it...or care to believe it, for that matter. How much did she actually know? There was no way either she or Allie would go anywhere near the slaughterhouse. He couldn't just say he was only hunting because he wouldn't have to sneak out of the house to do that.

He tried to choose his next words selectively when Allie walked over and broke the silence by saying, "Me and Jamie need refills." She grabbed Jamie's arm in the process and started dragging her away.

"Are you fucking kidding?" was all Gunner could exclaim.

* * *

The beat-up white pickup truck finally turned onto highway 42, the last road before they pulled up to Gunner's house. He sat in the passenger seat, his sunken and glassy eyes lazily gazing out the window. The young man downed what was left of his mixed drink from a clear soda bottle. It helped ease the tension on these long drives to and from the Canadian border.

He and his friend, Robbie, would take turns driving during the five-hour journey. They each worked two weeks on and then usually got a week off to do as they pleased before having to do it all over again. The two of them always drove one vehicle and split the cost of gas to try and be somewhat economical. They were making decent money for being twenty-one and only having high school educations, but it was getting to be a bit of a burden, always living in two places and spending all this time on the endless stretches of road together.

Gunner closed his eyes, but there was no way he was going to fall asleep. They were almost back, and since neither person was a very big talker, the music was usually cranked a few decibels above conversation level. He never really minded, especially since Robbie had a similar taste in music. It was probably better that he didn't fall asleep because he might have had a hard time waking up after consuming a very strong mixed drink.

The tired young man found himself thinking about Jamie during most of the drive home. He was looking forward to hearing her giggle and feeling her fingers gently run through his hair. There was something soothing about lying next to her and feeling as though he didn't have a care in the world. It was strenuous being away from her for a long duration of time, but they frequently texted and talked to each other each day. He found himself longing to see her face when he would listen to her soft voice tell him about her day, wanting to see the excitement of finding a new pair of shoes on sale, or disappointment of having to stay late to catch up at work instead of just hearing about it through the phone. He always tried to imagine what her alluring green eyes looked like when she was talking to him.

Before he knew it, Robbie was turning into his driveway. Gunner pulled out his phone and grunted when he looked at the blank screen. Jamie usually texted him on the day he came home. She hadn't messaged him for a few days, and they had only talked briefly the night before, but she knew he was coming home today. He decided to give her the benefit of the doubt and assume she was busy with work or school.

Robbie turned down the music and said, "One of us is going to have to learn to fly and buy a fucking plane."

Gunner just laughed and said, "Or fix up an old bus, put some couches in there, and have some dude named Jeeves chauffeur us to and from."

Robbie gave a tired smile and said, "That would be magical. Well, my kingdom awaits, and I need a beer. See you on the flip side, dude."

Gunner replied, "I'll shoot you a message later in the week," and grabbed his stuff. Robbie gave a friendly tap on his horn and hastily drove away.

The young man shuffled up the steps and opened the door to the duplex. He was instantly greeted by a pulsating rap beat. He could hear high pitched voices coming from the kitchen in between lyrics of the song that was playing on the computer in the living room. Gunner gave a loud sigh and cringed at the thought of having to entertain some guests.

He reluctantly made his way toward the kitchen. He peeked his head in the entryway and noticed Jamie and Allie sitting at the table with half a bottle of vodka and soda. They were both in full make-up and well-dressed from head to toe. Somehow, Gunner didn't think they were preparing to welcome him home.

"What's going on?" Gunner yelled over the music from the living room.

"Oh, it's just Jan," Allie said as she picked up her phone.

Jamie hesitantly got up and walked over to Gunner. "How was the trip?" she asked nonchalantly.

Gunner simply replied, "Fine," and continued walking down the hallway to their bedroom.

He threw his bag on the floor and started taking things out of his pockets to place on the dresser. Jamie came and stood in the doorway.

"Allie and I are going out for dinner and just a few drinks. I didn't know if you had eaten yet, but you can come if you want."

Gunner clenched his jaw slightly and replied, "It's been a long day, and I kind of thought it was just going to be me and you tonight. I only have until next weekend, as usual."

He watched her fidget with her shirt sleeves as she stood awkwardly in the doorway. "Well, we're just going to have a few drinks and then come back," she lied.

Gunner quickly replied, "Whatever, I'll find something else to do tonight."

Jamie stood there silently for a few seconds before Allie yelled down the hallway for her to come look at something on her phone. Jamie gave an apologetic look and said, "Well, we gotta go soon. People are waiting on us. It's just hard to make plans when you're away all the time." Then she abruptly disappeared.

Gunner sat in the bedroom, stunned for a while after the two girls had left. He was trying to process what had just happened while sobering up. After letting the initial shock subside, he decided to make his way to the kitchen and grab a bottle of whiskey from one of the cabinets. A stiff pour swirled around the bottom of the glass while he pulled out his phone. The seething young man typed a very long, crass message to vent all his frustrations. He let his thumb hover above the Send button for a few seconds, staring at the recipient's name for what seemed like an eternity. Any other day, he would have impulsively pressed the button and dealt with the repercussions later. For whatever reason, he decided to erase the message and simply send "we need to talk" to Robbie instead.

* * *

Allie continued walking toward the barn but turned her head and said, "Maybe you can invite your lady friend to come back. She seemed really interested in your whereabouts."

Gunner's eyebrows shot up in a furrowed crease. "What lady friend? What the fuck are you talking about?" He was afraid something like this might become quiet speculation if he neglected to be circumspect, but he hadn't planned on anyone else actually taking an interest in his whereabouts. Allie must have been bluffing.

"Tell him, Jamie," Allie demanded. Jamie just stood silently, staring at her cup. Allie got impatient and blurted, "Ugh, that lady cop Macy, or Mary, or whatever, Renard walked around pretending to make sure people were being responsible. She started asking about you, though. It was weird because she wasn't even in uniform."

Gunner closed his eyes and gave a loud sigh. "You can check my phone. I barely know her. I don't know what to tell you other than I don't know what the hell you're talking about. She's probably had it out for me based on what Stansby has told her."

It was a bit of a performance, but it was the best he could do without telling the whole story. It would have to suffice, for now. Besides, this new development was out of his control, and he needed time to fully comprehend the significance of the situation.

"Well, we're here to actually have a good time," Allie said with a sneer. She had a look on her face like she was plotting something dubious. They really didn't seem to know about what was in the slaughterhouse. That's really all Gunner cared about at the moment. He would have to deal with this later. It was obviously pointless to try and reason with either of the girls right now.

"Okay, well, I'm just going to leave. These parties aren't really my thing," Gunner replied. "Fuck this," he declared as he abruptly turned and walked back toward the smoldering pile of branches.

The young man sort of half trotted down the gravel driveway and back toward the direction of his SUV. He didn't feel much like staying to chat with anyone, even if he would have been in a cheerier mood. He just wanted to try to get to the bottom of whoever was messing with him.

Gunner was starting to think it was kind of a weird coincidence that Officer Renard had come up in conversation, considering their brief interaction earlier in the day. He didn't really know that much about her, except that she was relatively new and wanted to impress Stansby. Maybe someone had tipped her off about his whereabouts the night before. Had someone actually seen him in the woods? Maybe they had caught his license plate.

The young man got a creeping shiver as he pictured someone watching from a distance, stalking him like he had stalked the wolf. Someone may have spotted his vehicle and called in the plates thinking it was abandoned on the side of the road. But someone more than likely would have contacted him about that by now.

Gunner shook his head as he walked down the shadowy gravel road. The noise of the party began to fade in the distance, and the symphony of cricket chirps began their crescendo. He was tired and starting to get paranoid. The irritable young man decided he needed a way to slow his thoughts down. Otherwise, it would be like trying to catch a million butterflies in a tiny net. He pinched the bridge of his nose and tried to focus on the present task of walking to his SUV.

Before he knew it, Gunner was at the tail end of the slithering train of vehicles. His was still last in line, but the curious man noticed a dim light shining through the windshield. He cautiously approached the driver's side, slowly creeping on his toes so as not to make a lot of noise.

As he crept closer, Gunner noticed the cab light was on. One of the doors must have been open. The young man started to relax his shoulders a bit upon realizing what the source of the light was. He gave a bit of a laughing sigh, knowing he was working himself up over nothing. In his haste to blend into the thicket of trees, he must not have shut the door all the way. Just to be safe, the hunter casually checked his surroundings.

There was no sign of anyone else in the area, so Gunner peeked in the windows of the SUV. He shrugged his shoulders and pulled the door handle. It gave a full click and resisted the latch. Gunner paused for a moment and then slammed the door shut. The cab light was still on.

A nauseous feeling started to rise in the young man's stomach. He walked to the back of the SUV and pulled the latch of the back door. There was no click, and the door swung wide open after he barely touched it. He immediately slammed the door shut. The cab light went off.

* * *

Jamie let Allie drag her by the arm back toward the barn. She looked over her shoulder but knew Jan had made up his mind to leave and wasn't coming back. He had practically sprinted in the other direction. She also knew Allie had a way of getting under his skin, but he seemed even more irritable than normal during their little squabble. He was almost frantic.

She pulled out her phone and read his text again.

Just give me the fucking address

Jamie hadn't intentionally ignored his calls, but she wasn't in a hurry to talk to him after listening to his voicemail and reading his crass text message. He was always quick to get upset, but it had been a while since he had acted with such indignation. She knew she had been childish by trying to start a fight through text, but she hadn't expected this kind of visceral reaction.

She glanced at the squalid structure beyond the glow of the bonfire and wished the flames would just swallow it and put it out of its misery. A herd of people kept filing in and out as if it were housing some sort of carnival attraction. The bearded lady was probably lying in the basement drooling with a needle stuck in her arm.

Jamie had the sudden urge to just slide into her own bed and wrap herself in a burrito made of freshly washed sheets. Her thumb twitched as she contemplated calling Jan and apologizing, but he probably wouldn't even answer. She imagined him ripping open his car door and carelessly tossing his phone on the passenger side floor before speeding off down the gravel road. His taillights would be nothing but an evaporated red blur by the time his little tantrum ended, and he'd decide to give a shit where his phone had landed. The memory of when she found his secret stash of half-empty bottles of whiskey in the garage and confronted him about it abruptly smacked her like a tidal wave crashing against the rocky coastline.

"Did you hear what I said?" Allie asked.

Jamie looked at her and tried to piece together what she had just said, but the blank stare must have given her away. Allie impatiently rolled her eyes and repeated, "These guys said they're gonna go score some Molly, and asked if we wanna go with. They're worried that the cop lady might come back even though Remmy said he's known her since high school. Anyway, we'd only be gone for like a half hour tops. They said it's right down the road."

Molly did have a way of putting Jamie's mind at ease, even if the euphoria only lasted for an hour or two. She tried to remember the last time she had taken it. Jan never popped pills, so it would have been before they were together. That meant she probably hadn't taken it since freshman year of college.

"We don't even have a vehicle," Jamie replied. "Does that mean we'd have to pile into someone's car?"

"One of the guys has a truck we can squeeze into. Anyone who doesn't fit in the cab can ride in the back."

There were four guys standing in the barn, so that would mean at least six people would be going. Jamie didn't see any other women in the vicinity, and she barely knew anyone at this party. She wondered what picture would be used on the news if she squeezed between some random drunk guys in a back woods pickup truck and disappeared down a desolate gravel road, never to be heard from again. "Can't they just bring a few pills back?" she asked as optimistically as she could.

Allie couldn't hold back a deflated groan before responding, "I can try to convince them, but we might need to give them some money." She edged her way back over to the group of guys and tried to insert herself into the conversation.

As Jamie waited at the front of the barn, she felt her phone vibrate in her hand. Maybe Jan was trying to land one last jab before throwing his phone into obscurity. She almost decided to put her phone back into her pocket without reading the message, but she knew curiosity would gnaw at her as the night wore on.

Hey! Just checking in. I know it's the weekend of the big festival. Hope you're having fun. Miss you!! Love, Mom

Jamie just smiled as she read the message again. She looked at the time on her phone as it hovered on the screen above the picture of the sparkling blue ocean. It must be around seven o'clock on the West Coast, so Evelyn was probably taking her after-dinner stroll.

Jamie missed taking those walks with Evelyn, even the ones that were cut short because of swirling white flurries that would pelt their red faces during January snowstorms. They usually just wandered around town and discussed the latest gossip or the events of each other's day, but it was during those walks that Jamie learned of how her father and Evelyn first met. She also learned what life was like growing up in a small rural community during the politically charged sixties, what it tasted like to sip red wine for the first time on a vineyard in Napa Valley, and what to really expect on the highly anticipated prom night. It was an activity in which only the two of them were allowed to participate, even during holidays and special events.

Evelyn had always said that, even when she was pregnant with Jamie, she would take a short walk after dinner and talk to her belly. When Jamie was a fussy baby and wouldn't lie down for her nap, Evelyn would strap her in the stroller and walk her around the block. By the time Jamie was a toddler, it had become as routine as making coffee with breakfast. As the years passed by and Jamie eventually left the nest, Evelyn continued to religiously take those walks, even if it was by herself.

Some people found inner peace and mindfulness with yoga or mediation, but Evelyn found hers during those walks in the evening. She said they allowed her to clear her mind and recharge her batteries, especially when she was stuck on a problem or burned out on a freelance project from one of her difficult clients. The walks also gave her clarity on her relationships, particularly how to deal with Rob's shortcomings or Jamie's need for independence during her late teenage years. The walks were a boon, and a curse rolled up into one harmonious package.

Jamie began typing a response, but her finger wandered over to the phone icon. She didn't mean to press it, but her phone began dialing Evelyn's number. She put the phone to her ear and listened while the connection was being established. After a slight pause, a grainy ring rattled through the speaker. Jamie wasn't sure what she was going to say, but she forced herself to hold back a tear from streaming down her cheek.

CHAPTER SEVEN

A plethora of tools and seemingly insignificant objects were hastily strewn upon the kitchen table. The kitchen looked as if it had been caught in the rippling wake of a sudden storm. Cabinets were wide open, drawers were barely hanging on their tracks, and the floor was marked by dirt scuffs and a few remnants of dry and decayed leaves.

Gunner had driven straight home from the bonfire party. He was now fidgeting in a kitchen chair with a look of deep concentration. His fingers kept slipping as he exhaustively tried to pry his SIM card out of his cell phone.

The hunched over young man kept wiping his fingers on his pant leg in between shakes of his knee. The card was stuck in place under a thin metal bar that was firmly clasped around it, cuffing it to the phone. It was impossible to pull it out with short fingernails, so Gunner reached for a pair of pliers.

He was finally able to rip the SIM card away from the metal bar but left considerable scratch marks on it in the process. "Fuck it," Gunner yelled as he clamped the cover of his lifeless phone back on and buried it in his pocket. He wrapped the SIM card and battery in a plastic grocery bag and buried them in his other pocket. He threw the pliers on the table and went over to one of the open drawers.

He started frantically digging through the drawer but then walked to a cabinet when he remembered he needed an emergency flashlight. When he found it, he scrambled back over to the drawer but forgot why he had been searching it. He glanced at the table and then felt his pockets. Burner phone! He resumed digging through the clutter in the junk drawer until he found an old prepaid phone he had originally bought in case of an emergency.

They didn't own a land line, so Gunner thought the cheapest thing to do was to buy a burner phone as a backup plan. Neither of them had ever had to use it, so the minutes were still serviceable. In fact, he'd almost forgotten it was buried in the bottom of the kitchen drawer. He powered it up and brought it to the messy pile of tools on the table.

The frenzied man grabbed one of his larger hunting packs and brought it over to the table too. A brief look of disarray crossed his face as he tried to decide what tool should go where. He grabbed the flashlight and put it in one of the side compartments of the hunting bag. The binoculars were thrown in the other side compartment. Everything else was brushed with his arm into the main compartment. He had everything from gloves to pliers, knives, and rope.

Once the bag was zipped shut, Gunner grabbed a black hoodie and walked out the back door. He briskly walked to the garage and picked up the rest of his tools. He walked down the driveway to the passenger door of his vehicle and tossed his bag on the seat.

The young man opened his toolbox and pulled out a

screwdriver, hammer, and wire cutter. He then proceeded to open the dashboard of his vehicle and begin searching for a small rectangular box. Anybody could tap into a GPS system and track it if they knew what they were doing. If somebody really was following Gunner, he was going to make sure they couldn't tail his vehicle anymore. They would have to find him some other way.

He sifted through all the components and wires until he found the section he was sure was transmitting the GPS signal. It's amazing how basic and unadorned technology can be when it's stripped down and analyzed as a process with individual pieces that work together to achieve an end result. It's kind of like seeing an incredible magic trick and then being shown how the magician performs it.

Gunner clipped the wires and tossed the clippers back into the toolbox. He then hurriedly began putting his dashboard back together, but the damn thing wouldn't fit the way it was supposed to. He would push one side, and the other would pop out of place. He tried to use his knee to hold one side, but the space he was working in was too cramped. Finally, the exasperated man slammed the dashboard and punched the headrest of the passenger seat.

After the outburst, he sat hunched on his knees and panted heavily. Sweat started to drip off his forehead, so Gunner stepped outside the vehicle and discarded the hoodie. He then cracked his neck and stretched his tired fingers. His nerves felt like they were slowly burning on a hot steel grate. The crisp wind helped a little, but it was like blowing on a hot bowl of soup.

After a few moments of rest, the young man resumed putting the dashboard back together. This time he started from the middle and worked his way to the edges. It ended up looking a little crude, but he was finally able to get it back in place. Feeling like the job was somewhat satisfactory, Gunner tossed the rest of his tools in the box and brought them back to the garage.

He threw the toolbox on the floor and walked over to his gun rack. The gun he had used last night wasn't in its place. In his haste to skin the wolf hide, the irresponsible hunter must have laid it down somewhere. He knew it wasn't in the SUV because he had checked earlier. "Fuck!" he yelled. It could be anywhere.

Gunner walked outside and searched around the garage. He wondered if maybe he had left it against the wall but had no luck. He looked across the lawn at the slaughterhouse. It was probably in there, but the lamp used to light the decrepit structure and the key to unlock it was in the house. He thought about the wolf. If anyone actually knew what he was hiding in there, it could cost him his hunting license and his freedom. Adding a felony poaching offense to aggravated assault charges, property damage, and other gross misdemeanors would be a very serious matter.

The young man decided he would look for the weapon in the daytime. Jamie or Allie wouldn't touch it if they stumbled upon it, and there weren't any nosy kids around the house. Gunner decided to go back into the garage and grab a similar, less powerful rifle.

He placed the weapon in its case, put the strap over his shoulder, and brought it out to his vehicle. He mindlessly opened the back door and laid the rifle on the floor underneath the bloody blanket. Without hesitation, he slammed the door shut, climbed in the driver's seat, and promptly disappeared into the night.

* * *

A zig-zag pattern of footsteps left a prominent trail in the gravel that lay on the side of a quiet highway. Gunner had decided to leave the bar and wander in the general direction of the duplex. He was in no condition to drive the four miles home, but he wasn't in a very sociable mood either.

Evelyn had informed Jamie that she was going to live with her sister in California for a while as a way to clear her head and work out the issues involving Rob. Jamie thought it was probably a good idea, but she didn't want to live so far away from her mother. Her lease with Gunner was up at the end of summer, so she was contemplating going too.

A soundtrack of Jamie's voice was looping over and over in Gunner's head as gravel slid beneath his shoes. Her voice had been high-pitched and forced when she talked about the plan to crash at her aunt's house for a few months. It was only going to be until her mother was settled and feeling stronger.

There was no way the young man could afford to move to California right then, especially if the duration were uncertain. The beautiful beaches and enticing rays of year-round sunshine would be enough to lure anyone who had ever endured the hardship of a harsh winter. In fact, it would be nothing but a tease to bask in the ambiance of a balmy winter for a few weeks. The gentle crashing of ocean waves would constantly beckon a weary soul to return.

The tree branches along the highway creaked as Gunner thought about the studio and one-bedroom apartments around the area. Everything was so damned expensive, and all of the leases were twelve months. He noticed the stars weren't very bright tonight, but they probably were in California. Rent out there would be double or even triple what it was around here.

The gravel kept spraying across the blacktop and tall grass. The moon was only a small crescent this evening. Jamie would be taken care of if she went. Evelyn definitely needed to get away. How did people just move to California on a whim? What did people do for work when they got there? The highway seemed to stretch into a vast nothingness. There was nobody else here. "It will only be for a few months." The crickets chirped. How much further was it to the duplex? "Just until Mom is strong again." Something scurried into the tall grass. The highway was full of cracks and tar patches. "My aunt has a place in California." The yellow lines were uneven. The air was heavy. "I don't even know if I'll like it there." The gravel crunched. The trees swayed.

Suddenly Gunner looked up and approached a sizable bridge. It wasn't much to look at and almost blended into the silhouette of trees from a distance. The river that ran beneath it was swift and humming loudly. He walked to the side rail and stared at the rippling sway of a slithering tail of water. A tiny glint of moonlight would flicker on the top of a crest every so often. The continuous flow was mesmerizing and made the young man feel serene. The black water looked so peaceful as it pulsated to a steady cadence. He wanted to not only touch it but be a part of it.

Gunner climbed over the rusted guardrail and descended to a deteriorated beam below the bridge. Small flakes of rust floated off Gunner's hands as he tried to position himself over the water. His heartbeat was pulsing in his chest. The young man felt awake as he stood at least thirty feet above the swift current.

Gunner closed his eyes and just listened to the alternating rhythms of his heartbeat and the river current. It would only take a few seconds to reach the water. His head was swimming with alcohol, and it already felt like it was underwater. His hands slipped a little bit as he entertained the idea of falling freely through the air. The water would welcome him with open arms and cleanse him. The young man could feel his body start to bend forward.

Gunner just needed a little extra to make the world disappear. He wanted to melt away, forget he existed. He reveled in the idea of feeling completely numb. He wanted to go to a place where he didn't have a care in the world. That liberating feeling of knowing nothing really matters in the end. It was that delicate balance between philosophical bliss and reckless abandon.

As he stood motionless on the edge of the beam, he suddenly thought of the house in which he grew up. It was the only place he had ever really thought of as home. He hadn't been back there since his father had passed, but the idea of it enhanced his sense of euphoria.

For the next fifteen minutes, the world continued

to move at its usual pace. The crickets chirped. The tree branches moved back and forth. The clouds drifted over the crescent moon. The river hummed to its unwavering beat. But time stood perfectly still for Gunner.

* * *

The SUV sat behind a few tall trees next to a grassy clearing. Gunner had carefully turned off the main road and driven about two hundred feet over the naturally rough terrain. He tried to make sure he was tucked away in an inconspicuous location away from the main road. He was satisfied he had driven deep enough into the woods that no one would be able to spot his vehicle from the highway.

He knew the landscape fairly well, considering he had spent the last few weeks making sure he'd be able to track the wolf without the risk of getting caught trespassing. He had a very good idea of where the property lines intersected. There were some empty fields of amber cornstalk stumps that were part of the same property on the other side of the highway. The only other property within a mile was on the other side of the grassy clearing, deeper into the woods. That was the direction the other person had been heading this morning.

The hunter had methodically combed the edge of the clearing. There were no tire tracks or traces of a second person. Whoever was out this morning had more than likely acted alone. He or she must have been out hunting or gathering firewood and maybe stumbled upon Gunner's little transgression. It was odd that they were out at the early stages of dawn, but nonetheless, it was the only explanation that made sense to Gunner. There was nobody else in the area at that time, and nobody else lived in the immediate area.

The person was probably looking to extort Gunner, but the young man had no idea what they would be after besides money. He wanted to get a jump on the situation and try to find out what he was dealing with. If nothing else, he wanted to understand what the hell was going on. Why would someone just toss a note that said, "I saw you in the woods?" If it was to get under his skin, it had worked like a charm. They would have contacted the authorities by now if they were genuinely concerned about the law being broken, so it had to be something more than that.

With his bag strapped to his back and gun slung over his shoulder, the curious man ventured along the edge of the clearing and cautiously entered the crepuscular sea of mangled branches. The underbrush was thick, but there was a fresh trail of broken limbs and misplaced leaves along the forest floor. The person must have been in a hurry because the path was all over the place and didn't follow a particular direction. In fact, the trail even went sideways and backwards a few times.

The young man anxiously crept through the gnarled path as he weaved his way in the direction of the property. His body was washed over with a heightened sense of euphoria. He'd had the same feeling when he and his father tracked their first fox. The thrill of the unknown mixed with the anticipation of finding the den was exhilarating. He remembered feeling such a powerful sense of control. The difference was that they tracked the fox during the day so they could see the light pawprints in the soft mud.

Gunner slowly followed the trail for about twenty minutes until he came to a gravel access road. He was sure this road led up to the driveway of the only house in the area. The trail of broken branches ended here, so the person must have taken the road the rest of the way home.

The young tracker didn't want to leave himself exposed on the open road, even in the cover of night, so he stayed within the tree line as he followed the road around a bend. As he made his way around the corner, Gunner took off his bag and dug for his binoculars. When he found them, he put them up to his eyes and scanned the distance. Sure enough, he spotted a dead end to the access road that led to a driveway.

The mailbox was at the entrance of the access road near the highway, but Gunner knew it belonged to a J. Emerson. A little research on the Internet provided a few more details about Mr. Emerson. According to his social media profiles, Jerrod was his first name, he was thirty-two, and he had been a bartender at one point in time. There was no indication he was married or had any kids, so hopefully, he lived alone.

Gunner waited for a few minutes and listened to his surroundings. It was eerily quiet. The only light was cast from the moon and a few stars that scattered across the treetops. He didn't even see any traces of an aura coming from beyond the driveway. Signs pointed to nobody being home.

The young man put his binoculars back in his bag and strapped it on his back. He began inching his way toward the front of the driveway. Slowly but surely, the house came into view. It was difficult to make out the shapes of the house from this distance, but there were definitely no lights on.

Gunner took out his binoculars again and looked at the property. He spotted a place in the grass where leaves had been displaced, and the trail had resumed. The intrigued man sat and contemplated his options. He had come this far but now had more questions than answers. What the fuck was he really going to accomplish if he went any further? If he turned around and went back, there would be no harm, and nobody would even know he had been here. But nothing would get resolved, and his paranoia would surely get the best of him. It would only be a matter of time before Stansby showed up asking about the dead wolf in the slaughterhouse.

It had occurred to him to just get rid of the wolf and any evidence he had been poaching, but he didn't know what kind of pictures would surface in a text message on his phone if and when someone was going to extort him. He might as well have taken a selfie with the dead wolf draped over his shoulders. Gunner didn't want to risk the chance of getting that anonymous text or phone call, and something was telling him that this wasn't a bluff or a joke. He decided to trust his instincts. Jerrod Emerson needed some further investigation if only to eliminate him as a tormentor.

* * *

Jamie thanked the Lyft driver for the ride and slammed the passenger door of the blue Prius. The engine hummed to life as the driver pulled away from the driveway and drove in the direction of his next fare. His night was just getting started, but Jamie had already had enough of the Harvest Moon Festival.

Allie had abandoned her at the party to go with those guys to score some Molly. Jamie wasn't at all surprised or upset, considering the call with her mother had lasted over thirty minutes. She eventually told Allie she was getting a headache and some intense cramping as an excuse to call it a night, so they both decided to go their separate ways. At least Allie knew most of the guys huddled near the barn, so Jamie didn't feel quite as guilty calling it an early night.

At first, the nostalgic thought of popping those pills had excited her, but the feeling quickly faded after she began to sober up. It might have been different if it was just the two of them sitting in the comfort of one of their houses, but that wasn't going to be an option tonight. It was one thing to gather around a bonfire with a bunch of acquaintances and strangers to have a few drinks and celebrate the festival, but it was something entirely different to leave with a four-to-one ratio of strange men to take drugs on a lonely gravel road in an unfamiliar truck. Jamie knew she would have wasted the high trying not to appear overly anxious.

She was glad her mother had answered the phone when she called. Evelyn had been finishing a walk along the pier and paused to "watch another spectacular sunset sparkle on top of the water," as she put it. Jamie could hear the splashing of the ocean waves as she listened to her mother talk enthusiastically about a new client she was working with. She also revealed she had earned enough money to start looking for her own place, which had been long overdue.

As Jamie walked up her driveway, she tried to remember the last time she had visited her mother. Evelyn usually flew home for major holidays and Jamie's birthday in July, but Jamie couldn't remember the last time they had flown to California. It was always more difficult than it needed to be because her aunt had limited space, so they needed to rent a place when they went to visit. Jan hated to spend the money, especially with the added cost of airline tickets, so what was supposed to be a cheerful planning experience always ended in a fight.

Jamie's train of thought was rudely interrupted when she looked up and noticed the garage door was open. Jan's yellow toolbox was lying in the empty space where the SUV was usually parked. The cover was wide open, and a few screwdrivers were standing on the edge like somebody had carelessly tossed the toolbox after they couldn't find what they were looking for.

The first alarming thought that popped into Jamie's head was that somebody had broken into their garage, but then she remembered how frantic, almost manic, Jan had been at the party. She contemplated calling him, but there was a slim chance he would actually answer. The side door to the garage was still locked, so the potential thief would have had to have known the garage door code to get in, which was highly unlikely. It looked like all the tools were there, so nothing seemed to be stolen.

Jamie slid the toolbox against the wall and punched in the code to close the garage door. She waited for it to clunk shut before turning around and walking toward the back door of the house. She stopped midway in the grass when she noticed the kitchen light was on.

An uneasy feeling began to fester in the pit of her stomach. Jan was always good about turning the lights off before he left, wherever he had gone. He always closed the garage door, too, even if he knew she was home. Something about tonight was off, yet strangely familiar.

Jamie crept closer to the house and peeked through the kitchen window. She felt weird peeping into the window of her own home, but she decided it would be better to be safe than sorry. The window was a small square above the sink, so it was difficult to see much of anything besides the walls. It didn't look like anybody was in there, so she gathered her courage and walked up to the door.

Her hand shook as she jiggled the knob. She felt a slight reprieve from anxiety when she realized it was locked. At least Jan had had the wherewithal to lock the house before jetting off to God knows where, so maybe he hadn't become completely unhinged. She just wished she knew what had set him off like this. The thought of trying to pry it out of him tomorrow morning made her exhausted, even more so than she already felt.

All she wanted to do now was shower the bonfire smoke off her body and curl up in bed with a trashy novel, so she reached into her purse and grabbed her keys. As she pushed the door open, she dropped her keys and put her hand to her mouth. She tried to hold back tears as her eyes darted around the chaos that was spread about the kitchen.

She had been able to see the tops of the empty chairs from the window, but not the kitchen table or the countertops. It looked like the contents of one of the drawers had been flung everywhere in a fit of rage. Most of the drawers were barely hanging on their tracks, and the cabinets had been left flung wide open. The countertops were littered with junk like batteries, rubber bands, and other stuff that rarely saw the light of day. The laptop had been knocked onto one of the chairs, its dangling cord ripped away from the wall.

Deja vu sucker-punched Jamie in the gut. She had witnessed this scene before but in a different place. She remembered waking up in an empty bed one morning when they were married on what she had thought was a normal autumn Saturday morning. The last thing she had remembered from the night before was getting home from the bar with Jan and going straight to bed. She thought he had come to bed and maybe gotten up early to take care of stuff around the house, so she didn't think much of it at the time.

The first thing she noticed when she made it downstairs around eight was how drafty the house had felt. There were no embers smoldering in the fireplace or the smell of freshly brewed coffee wafting in the air. Jan's keys had been sitting on the counter, and his coat was still hanging on the wall.

She remembered how quickly the panic had set in. She had walked around the house calling his phone a few times to see if maybe he had fallen asleep somewhere odd, but there had been no trace of him. She had felt like she was being stabbed a little harder every time the call went to voicemail, so she had eventually put her phone down and tried to think rationally.

Then it had hit her all at once. She remembered

the date. That morning had been the grim anniversary of when Frederick had passed. She had completely forgotten because Jan never brought it up and certainly never discussed it willingly.

For whatever reason she still didn't fully understand, Jamie had decided to check one last place: the garage. It was where Jan would always go when he needed to be by himself after they had first been married. She found out why when she went to find him.

Jamie found him passed out cold on the garage floor, lying on his side with the hood from his sweatshirt pulled around his head. An empty bottle of whiskey was cast aside, but the glass was still intact. The door to the gun locker hung open, and a heap of hidden liquor bottles that had presumably been rummaged through during the early morning hours were overflowing onto the garage floor. The normally immaculate workbench was in disarray. Every single tool Jan owned was lying next to a fresh dent in the wood.

Now, as she stared at the mess in the kitchen, that nauseating feeling of helplessness embraced her with icy arms. She remembered how painstakingly difficult it had been to clean up the mess in the garage that one fateful morning. There was no way she could clean up another one, so she angrily locked the back door, turned off the kitchen light, and went upstairs to shower.

CHAPTER EIGHT

The house sat silently at the end of the gravel driveway. Gunner scanned the premises for any yellowed or bare patches of grass. Even though it was difficult to clearly see the yard at night, there didn't seem to be any signs of a dog. There was no kennel, but the trail of scattered leaves led to a homemade shed on the right side of the house.

The yard was unkempt and filled with random objects. The lawn looked like it hadn't been mowed in weeks, and tree branches and leaves were littered everywhere. There were stacks of pallets by the shed and cinder blocks spread in random places. The remains of an old classic Cadillac were deposited in the backyard. It had probably been a beautiful machine in her younger days, but now it was reduced to a rusted frame and missing doors with half a tarp thrown over her to spare her last shred of dignity. There was also a newer black truck that was oddly parked on the lawn next to the shed.

The house was nothing much to look at. The frames around the windows were weather-beaten and stripped. The front steps were broken and led to a front door that needed to be painted. The entire house looked like it was hunched over and sad like it had given up on life.

The anxious hunter drifted a little deeper into the woods and laid his rifle down under a log. He wanted to go onto the property for a closer inspection, and he wasn't about to trespass with a gun in his hand. There was no chimney on the roof and no evidence of any kind of fire pit in the yard. In fact, a fire may very well have been a hazard. So that would most definitely rule out somebody gathering firewood this morning.

The most likely scenario was that this guy had been hunting too, but there were no other shots fired. He must have been using illegal snares or something. Gunner didn't see any evidence of it, but this Emerson guy could have gone back and cleaned them up. If this guy had caught something large enough to drag through the woods, why didn't he just throw it in the back of his truck?

Then Gunner remembered getting pulled over this morning. Maybe it was better to be safe than sorry, but it was still sloppy for a hunter who would risk getting caught snaring wild animals. It didn't add up that he would drag an animal leaving a prominent trail to his house but have the wherewithal to go back and clean up his traps. The guy could have just panicked. Either way, someone knew Gunner's secret, so he was going to learn Emerson's secret.

The young man opened his bag, took out his knife, and put it in his back pocket. It was more of a utility knife than anything. He grabbed his flashlight, too, then zipped up the bag and laid it next to his rifle. He looked around for some distinguishing trees or marks so he could remember where he stashed his supplies. There was a tree with a hollowed-out center that kind of looked like a ship's porthole that would have to suffice.

Gunner gradually started meandering his way toward the house. Every fifty feet or so, he would pause and scan the area with his binoculars. The house still seemed desolate and silent. It was too dark to see through the windows. The only noise came from the leaves being crunched under the young man's boots. The air was light and cool, but there was no trace of wind.

After stopping and scanning about three times, Gunner finally made it to the edge of the tree line. The adrenaline was coursing through every vein in his body. He had to keep himself from sprinting to the shed. Now that he had paused again, the only sound came from his rapid breathing. It almost seemed deafening in his ears. The young man closed his eyes and lightly squeezed his right index finger toward his palm. His breathing started to slow back to normal after a few seconds, and he was able to compose himself.

The hunter took a deep breath and opened his eyes. The shed was about twenty-five meters straight ahead of him. He looked around the yard as he carefully made his way out from the comfort of the tree line, inching his way over the leaves and branches so as not to leave a trail of footsteps behind him. Halfway across the lawn, the young man decided to creep along the path of matted grass that led the rest of the way to the shed. He made it there in a matter of seconds, but it felt like an eternity.

Once near the shed, Gunner stood crouched with his hand against a wooden pallet and safely out of view from the peeping windows of the house. His head was pulsating, and he saw red dots floating around him. His heart felt like it was in his throat, but the young man embraced the rush and almost reveled in the moment. "This is absolutely insane," he muttered to himself. He felt his back pocket to make sure the knife and flashlight were still there.

When the initial high subsided, Gunner poked his head around the side of the shed. The truck was parked right next to the door of the small structure. Now that the hunter got a good view of the front of the truck, he noticed the left headlight was smashed, the front bumper was missing, the hood was slightly caved in, and the windshield had a large crack in it. Whatever it had run into had caused some serious damage. That could very well be the reason this Emerson guy didn't use it this morning.

Gunner almost crawled to the side of the truck and peeked inside. The interior was immaculate. There was no trace of paper or even dirt on the floor mats. In fact, the outside of the truck had been washed very recently too. The smell of some kind of cleaning agent was still very pungent. That was odd that the truck had been cleaned before getting repair done to the body. The confused man ran his fingers along the side and spied the back of the truck. There wasn't a trace of dust or dirt. Someone had hosed and wiped down every inch of the vehicle.

An uneasy tension started to wriggle inside of Gunner. This guy obviously wasn't a clean freak, given the nature of his yard and the outside condition of his house. Something must have been off about him. He had spent an unusual amount of time tediously caring for a broken truck, but the classic car sat untouched, withering away underneath a dirty tarp, and the house looked like it just wanted to collapse from exhaustion.

Gunner looked down at the ground and followed the matted path of grass with his eyes to the door of the shed. He thought of the wolf sitting in the slaughterhouse back home. What the fuck am I doing? he thought. *Just go get your things and go home. Get rid of the body and come up with a story. That's as much as you can control.*

Except the more the young man told himself that, the more apprehensive he became. His morbid curiosity wouldn't allow him to just turn around and go home. "I've come this far already," he told himself as he edged closer to the shed door. "Just do it, look inside."

Gunner lifted the latch, cringing as it squeaked. He paused and peered behind him. There were no lights or signs of any movement coming from the house. He turned back around and gently started opening the door. A triangle of pale moonlight slid across the dirt floor of the shed before the door got stuck on the ground halfway open. The young hunter didn't want to mess with the hinges, so he just decided to slip inside the small opening.

It was pitch black. Gunner nervously fumbled around in his back pocket for his flashlight. His breathing started to become erratic. When he finally found it, he flicked it on and shined it straight ahead. All he could see was a tiny circle of dirt. The structure seemed bigger from the inside. The whole floor was just dirt.

The young man started to shuffle his feet as he moved around a little bit. He stuck his hand out in front of him to keep from running into a wall. He could only see the tiny circle of light that was directly in front of him. He found a wall of the shed and moved alongside of it with his hand against it. So far, it was just dirt on the floor and a rough wooden wall.

As the young man slowly shuffled against the wall, his foot kicked something hard and knocked it over. He frantically waved the flashlight toward the floor. He stopped it when it reflected off something shiny. After briefly hesitating, Gunner reached down and picked it up. An immediate sense of dread invaded his body. He shifted the familiar weight of the rifle he used to shoot the wolf this morning in his hands. He didn't need to shine the flashlight over the entire weapon to know it was his. All he needed to do was feel it.

The panicked hunter started panting heavily. His teeth started grinding as he struggled to compose himself. *Why the fuck...? How did...?* he thought. He tried to breathe in, but his breath got caught in the back of his throat.

As the young man started to get worked into a frenzy, his shaking hand cast the small circle of light toward the back corner of the shed. It landed on the tarp and rope that he had seen being dragged into the woods at dawn. They were hiding a misshapen lump.

A sick feeling suffocated Gunner. He didn't feel like throwing up. He felt like his best friend had died, and he had no one else in which to confide. He lifted the gun and almost smacked it against his head. He let out a choked grunt through clenched teeth. His vision started to get blurry as tears of frustration welled in his eyes. "This can't.... Why is...? Fuck!" He tried to breathe out but could only inhale.

He dropped the gun and went over to the lump in the corner. He tapped it with his boot. It was stiff and unforgiving. Gunner wanted to just run out of that decrepit shed and not look back. He wanted to just run into the night and disappear. But instead, he slowly peeled back the tarp and stared at the blood-soaked brown hair and lifeless eyes of the missing girl from the news.

Everything went red as an unnatural screaming growl escaped Gunner's throat. "It...! But...!"

He screamed until his lungs were empty of air. His fists beat against the ground. He dug his fingers into the dirt and scratched until they bled. Then he nearly passed out next to his gun and flashlight and laid there until the red haze disappeared.

* * *

Gunner sat at the kitchen table, twirling his bronze six-month sobriety chip in his fingers. He was trying to remember the name of the guy who had presented it to him earlier that week. Adam? It was some guy who took it upon himself to try and get Gunner more involved in the program instead of just showing up and listening to other people talk during meetings. Allen? Whatever the dude's name was, he had the audacity to call him Jan as he presented the chip like it was the Nobel Peace Prize.

Jamie broke his meager concentration by walking into the kitchen talking on her phone. "That's great! I wish I could have seen it. What did you two do after that?" She had been spending at least an hour talking on the phone with Evelyn every day. The conversations were getting cheerier lately, so it seemed to be lifting her mood a bit.

The young man started spinning his medallion on the table, flicking it with his finger to keep the momentum going. He was finally starting to feel like his body was able to relax. For so long, he had felt on edge. Ever since his father passed, he hadn't been able to sit still or focus on anything.

Jamie glanced over and kind of turned in the opposite direction. "He's good. Things are starting to get better. We've both just kind of been doing our own thing lately. I don't want to interfere with his recovery plan." She never knew what to call his situation. She was trying to be supportive, but she didn't fully understand what her role was supposed to be.

Gunner wanted to open up about his father's death, the full extent of his drinking, the fragmented memories of his mother, but he wasn't ready yet. He was still too vulnerable. He couldn't bear any sort of rejection or sense of judgment right now. His mind was very fragile, and he just wanted to focus on the positives.

"Well, send me pictures. Maybe I can find a cheap flight out there in the next few months. I miss you guys." There was a long pause before she glanced in his direction again and said, "I will. I love you too. Bye."

Jamie held her phone in her hand and just disappeared for a few minutes, her eyes drifting along with the gray clouds outside the square kitchen window. Gunner flicked his medallion, and it fell off the table, hitting the floor with a loud ping. The sudden noise brought Jamie back to the kitchen. "Mom sends her love," she stated in his general direction.

"How is she doing?" Gunner asked, even though he had overheard some of the conversation and knew that not much had probably changed since yesterday.

"Good," she said as her face lit up slightly. "They went shopping at a new place near the South Beach.

She might send us something in a week or two, but she wouldn't say what."

"If it's one of those seashell necklaces again, I'm going to start making necklaces out of rocks that I find in the yard and send them in an insulated container with some snow."

This caught Jamie off guard, and she started to laugh. "Don't be mean. She means well. She's not trying to rub it in. As long as you don't use the necklaces for target practice."

"Damn. Well, what else am I going to do while I sit around in my overalls and straw hat on Saturdays?" he said with a smirk.

"We can strum our banjos," Jamie giggled. The brief sound of her giggle brought a smile to Gunner's face. It was a beautiful noise that almost seemed foreign to him these days.

Suddenly Gunner remembered hearing the soft stroke of piano keys through the floorboards of his childhood home. It was a beautiful sound that he only heard when his mother was having a cheery day. It would always bring a smile to his face as he sat on his bedroom floor and listened.

These repressed memories were coming back to him quite frequently over the last few months. Things that were buried for years had started crawling their way out of the crypts of his mind. The memories weren't decayed but actually extremely vivid. It was as if nostalgia was on steroids.

He looked over at Jamie and hesitated before asking, "Did I ever tell you my mother used to play the piano?"

Jamie gave a thoughtful glance and simply shook her head. It wasn't dismissive, but more like she didn't know how to respond. She stared at him, willing him to elaborate.

Gunner started to say something, but a bit of panic took hold of his voice. He waited a second so he could collect his thoughts. He wanted to hold on to this memory and never let it go. It was all his, and nobody could ever take it away from him. He also wanted Jamie to share a glimpse, but he didn't know how to describe it for her.

"Her favorite thing to practice was from a piece called 'Danse Macabre.' It's from an orchestral score that was written based on French superstition. Supposedly 'Death' appeared at midnight on Halloween and played his fiddle. The dead would dance for him until the rooster crowed at dawn. Then they would have to go back to their resting places until next year. I swear, my mother would try to capture every ounce of the celebration with every stroke of the key. I never knew what the piece was actually about until I was much older, but I always remembered how passionately she hit the keys."

Jamie just sat and listened, her body completely still. Gunner closed his eyes and tried to hold on to the memory with all his strength. He opened his mouth to continue describing what he had heard, but a loud bang came from the front of the house.

"Jamie! Oh my god, where are you? You need to hear this!" echoed a shrill voice.

The memory began to evaporate. Jamie gave an apologetic look before responding, "In the kitchen, Allie.

Don't you even knock anymore?" She kind of laughed and waited for the big news.

The young man got up and exited through the back door.

* * *

Gunner laid on the dirt floor until his breathing was back to normal. His throat was on fire, and his fingers were throbbing. A numbing chill ran up his spine, almost like the onset of hypothermia. He began mending the dirt where his fingers had dug so deeply. The flashlight was pointed toward the door of the shed, but he could still see the outline of the body. Her hollow face was burned into his memory.

The horrified man got up and walked to the heavy door. He peaked his head out to see if his outburst had woken anybody. As far as he could tell, no one was startled. The house was still hidden in shadows. There didn't even seem to be anyone home.

Gunner took his flashlight and held it in his mouth, then reached into his pocket and pulled out the burner phone. It was very basic, but it was still equipped with a tiny camera. He flipped it open and willed himself to walk to the back of the shed again.

It was almost surreal to see the outline of the tarp through the dark green phone screen. None of this could be real. He forced his other hand to quit shaking as he hovered over the body.

He had stood over countless animals that had had their lives cut short by his very hands, but it still hadn't prepared him for this. The apprehensive young man absentmindedly pulled the tarp back. This time he felt like throwing up, but he held it down and took a picture of the poor woman's face. Her body was contorted in a bit of a crumple, like a discarded mannequin. Gunner couldn't take it any longer, so he quickly covered her up and bolted out the shed door.

When he was back outside, he coughed feverishly as hot beads of sweat stung his eyes. He looked at the ground and couldn't see from his peripherals. It was like looking through a kaleidoscope, but without the colorful shapes. The young man tried to gather his bearings.

He still had the phone in his hand, so he checked his service. There were two bars, so he could call this in if he wanted. But how was he going to explain stumbling upon this with two of his rifles on the premises? As far as he could tell, she hadn't been shot with his rifle. So why the fuck was it here? Maybe he could just grab it and run back to his vehicle and call it in before anyone noticed.

A flicker of light caught the hunter's eye through the tree line. Too late — someone was quickly approaching in their car. Gunner panicked and slammed the shed door shut. He looked behind him and saw the headlights turn into the long driveway. He would never make it to the tree line in time. Pure trepidation made the young man's legs nearly glide over a few cinder blocks in the yard and dive into the backseat of the junked classic car. He was barely able to throw the tarp over himself before the headlights caught him in his tracks.

Gunner sat as still as he could with his shirt sleeves stuffed in his mouth. The tarp was still settling around him as he waited to hear a car door slam. He didn't hear anything. It was completely silent except for the pounding of his heartbeat. He strained his ears to listen intently. Still nothing. Could he have been seen? The car wasn't running, but he was sure nobody had gotten out yet. Dread lodged itself in the young man's throat. Maybe he should just make a run for it. He was fucked if he had been seen and continued to wait in his current position.

As he slowly took his sleeves out of his mouth, he heard gravel crunch underneath car tires. The engine turned off, and a car door opened. As it slammed shut, a second car door opened and slammed shut. There were two cars.

A distressed man's voice began to say, "What the fuck am I going to do? I thought you were going to help me take care of this. I could have done it by now if you would have stayed outta this and just watched my back."

An irritated woman's voice said, "Hold on. I'm stuck cleaning up your fucking mess again. You need to keep your shit together. If you hadn't been drinking, none of this would have happened. Looks like you didn't even try to hide what you did, for fuck's sake. I take it she's in the shed?"

The man replied, "Well, I would have buried her somewhere no one woulda found her, but you told me you had a better plan. And it's not like I coulda just thrown her in the back of the truck. After I got home and called you, the engine went to shit."

"You killed somebody this time, Jerrod! And people are already looking for her. I should have brought you into the station, but we both know if you go down, you'd take me with you. This is the last time—I'm done. I don't owe you shit after this!"

"Well, your plan is starting to unravel, Mary. I'm starting to panic. We don't even know if that lunatic saw anything. Who knows what that weird fucking loner was doing? He woulda said something by now, right?"

"We can't take that chance, especially now that you have his gun," she said.

"Well, you were supposed to keep an eye on him, but apparently, he fell off the grid," he retorted.

"I made sure he has something he'll have a hard time explaining in case he says anything, but you took matters into your own hands. We need a reason to go after him! Look, we can still deal with this. We just need to tweak the plan. Let's find a way to dispose of the body first. Then let's erase any trace she was ever within a mile of this place."

The two continued arguing as they disappeared into the house. Gunner heard everything he needed to know about the situation for now. It looked like going to the cops was definitely out of the question.

* * *

Jamie pumped her legs just short of breaking into a light jog. She was having a difficult time keeping up with her husband's torrid pace. His stride was much longer, so he could dodge the tangles of fallen brush much easier than she could.

As soon as he had parked the truck, he basically made a beeline for the wooded hillside. His gun, or rifle as he had corrected her, was comfortably slung over his left shoulder and pointed toward the canopy of green leaves. Jamie was tightly gripping the black strap of her rifle with both hands, always conscious of which way it shifted on her back while she tried not to fall flat on her face. Even though it wasn't loaded, she still wasn't completely comfortable carrying it yet.

"Hey Jan?" she wheezed in between heavy breaths. "Can we slow down a minute?" She could feel her ponytail becoming frizzy and loose, so she stopped to readjust her hair.

Jan looked back, and his eyes became wide. "Oh shit, didn't realize how far ahead I had gotten," he said as if he was sitting on the couch and not surging up a wooded hillside. "Take your time. It's just a little further," he said, shifting his strap for the first time.

Jamie pulled her hair back as tight as she could and tangled the elastic band around it. It was already damp, but she didn't mind. She stole a glance at Jan and watched him close his eyes and breathe in deeply like he was smelling a bouquet of freshly cut flowers.

She could feel a smile pulling at the corner of her mouth. It was invigorating to see that spark return to his eyes and the extra bounce in his step. It was a welcoming and refreshing change to that sullen black cloud that seemed to be constantly hovering above his head during the last seven months. The color had also returned to his skin, and his muscles had turned into rocks. Thick veins rippled through the beautiful tattoos on his forearms.

Jan had been spending most evenings attending AA meetings, going to the gym, or working later than usual. He had tried to explain that he needed the extra discipline and distraction from his old habits, but it still didn't make leftover meals for one taste any better. Jamie had been doing everything she could to be supportive, but Jan wasn't one to ask for help even if he needed it. So Jamie had done what she thought he needed most, which was to give him the space to figure things out in his own way.

Once she was able to catch her breath, she fiddled with the rifle strap until she could feel the weight of the weapon shift to the middle of her back. She wasn't entirely sure where they were heading, but that didn't matter. She was still in shock that Jan had invited her in the first place.

"Okay, lead on," she said as she caught up to him.

The sunshine did a playful little dance on her skin as they continued walking along a rutted dirt path that led deeper into the forest. A sing-song chatter echoed throughout the treetops as two birds chirped back and forth. If nothing else, the venture through the forest was shaping up to be a gratifying Saturday morning hike.

"Here we go," Jan exclaimed as he sped ahead of her. Jamie looked ahead and spotted a clearing through the trees. She saw a long bulky log lying at the edge, the center of it splintered and riddled with bullet holes.

Jan slung his rifle off his shoulder and laid it against the base of a tree. He then wiggled out of his green backpack and unzipped the top. His hand clanked around inside and reemerged with a few empty coffee cans, which he brought over to the bulky log. He took his time carefully arranging and spacing the cans as if they were a house of cards that might collapse from the slightest breeze.

"Gotta make sure they're properly spaced. Otherwise, they might knock into each other," he said as he stood up with a satisfied nod. He gave the log a half-hearted kick to make sure they didn't wobble off the side.

A few of the rusted blue cans shivered but didn't fall, so Jan went over to grab his rifle and stand near his wife.

"My dad and I would do this every Saturday right before hunting season started," he said as he pulled a box of bullets from his front pocket. "We would have a completion of sorts," he continued as he opened and inspected the bullet chamber of his rifle. He slid his finger around the opening and removed any extraneous residue.

Jamie left her rifle slung over her shoulder as she intently watched Jan's every movement and clung to his every word. He was so animated and focused on his methodical approach. She felt like any movement on her part would have disrupted his sacred ritual. She could almost see him mentally ticking off an imaginary checklist as he completed each step.

He slid the chamber closed with a sharp click and brought the butt of the rifle up to his shoulder. His eye narrowed down the sight as he gracefully swung the barrel toward each can in one sweeping motion. His finger clicked the trigger in rapid succession as he imagined popping each can off the log. His mind was beyond being in the zone. It was in a completely different stratosphere.

Jan surprisingly looked over at Jamie while still aiming at the log and said, "The competition would consist of distance and speed. If nothing else, it was a fun way to get our sights in order and ready for the season." The sweeping spray of imaginary bullets flew in the opposite direction this time.

Jamie mindfully slid her rifle off her shoulder and tried to discreetly examine the barrel. Her thumb brushed against the bullet chamber, but she didn't dare put any pressure on it yet. She looked down at the size of the bullets and wondered how four of them would be able to fit inside the chamber all at once.

As soon as Jan snapped out of his zone, he started laughing. "Only one bullet can fit in the chamber at once. The speed was more about how fast we could load and reload," he said as he shouldered his unloaded rifle again.

He walked over and put his hands on hers while gently guiding them toward the bullet chamber. His warm, firm touch felt so comforting on her clammy hands that she almost forgot she was holding a rifle for the first time in her life. He rested his chin on her shoulder as he patiently showed her how to open the chamber. She wasn't paying attention to any of the words that were coming out of his mouth, just the warmth and reassurance of being wrapped in his arms.

It reminded her of when they first got married, and she would sit curled between his legs on the couch while they watched a movie. She used to love the way his hands would start on her shoulders during the title scene and end up wrapped around her waist in a tight embrace by the closing credits. Sometimes the heat from the fireplace in the winter months would lull them both to sleep, and they would end up spending the night on the couch buried beneath a mound of blankets. She tried to remember the last movie they had watched together, but her mind was drawing a blank.

The swift, sharp click of the bullet chamber snapped her back to the forest, and she immediately dropped the rifle. It harmlessly fell to the ground, but she closed her eyes and tensed her shoulders as she waited for Jan's irritated groan. Instead, he gave her shoulders a brief squeeze and calmly bent down and picked up the rifle.

"That's why we don't load it until we're ready to shoot, and we always leave the safety on," he said as he pointed to the bright orange button on the side of the rifle.

Jamie felt her muscles ease and let out a sigh of relief. "That sounds like something your dad instilled in you at a young age," she said.

Jan's ears turned a slight shade of red, and he brushed his hand through his hair like he always did when he was embarrassed. "Yeah, that did sound just like him, didn't it?" His eyes moved back to the blue cans on the log. "He could have unloaded, reloaded, and probably popped off at least one of those cans blindfolded if he wanted to. But somehow, I always seemed to win our little competition."

The two stood silent for a moment and listened to the singsong chatter in the trees. Jamie felt like reaching for his hand, but both of hers were still firmly wrapped around the cold metal of her rifle. Instead, she asked, "When was the last time you both came out here?"

Jan furrowed his brow as he tried to remember. "Must have been when I was still in high school."

Jamie could have sworn she saw his face twitch into a brief cringe as soon as he said it, so she decided to leave the conversation alone. The rifle was beginning to feel heavy, so she looked around for a place to lean it.

Before she could set it down, she noticed a furry brown rabbit sitting just outside the clearing. It was tensely frozen in place, but it was watching their every move. Jamie had the urge to pet its fluffy fur, but she knew she'd never be able to approach it in the wild. She still wanted to admire it from afar, so she tried to gently set the rifle down with as little effort as possible. Unfortunately, the rabbit's survival instincts kicked in, and it darted into the safety of the underbrush as soon as she turned in its direction.

"You want to try shooting first?" Jan asked

Jamie looked at the spot where the rabbit had been and replied, "No, you go ahead. I'm not ready yet."

CHAPTER NINE

The thick fabric that was draped over Gunner began to stick to his exposed skin. He waited in darkness until he was absolutely sure no one else was outside. His knee was throbbing. He must have smacked it when he dove onto the cold, stiff seats. He was starting to get light-headed as he breathed onto the tarp. Fresh oxygen was sealed outside, so the weary man discreetly peeked his head from underneath the material.

Dingy yellow light leaked from one of the first-story windows on the side of the house. They must have been in one of the front rooms. Gunner couldn't see anything from the back window.

He needed to get out of there. The restless man looked around as far as his head could swivel. He couldn't seem to concentrate on what he was looking at. It was like he knew what everything was, but he forgot what it was called. His muscles started to shake as he waited for the shock to subside.

The young man breathed in deep, held it for four seconds, and slowly released the breath. He looked around again, and everything started to gradually make sense as it came back into focus. He still had a bit of tunnel vision, but he could see what was directly in front of him with clarity.

There weren't any trees in between him, the shed, and the house. Some overgrown shrubs in dire need of pruning grew along the side of the house, but they were only a few feet tall. They were wildly growing well below the bottom of the sunken-eyed windows. Junk was dispersed in random places of the backyard, but nothing large enough to hide a grown man. The remains of the car that Gunner was hiding in sat next to a maple tree that had shed most of its leaves, but it was the closest one to the back of the house.

He had two options. The first was to go back the way he had come. It would be the fastest, but there was no cover from his current position to the shed. He might also set off a motion sensor if he got too close to the house in order to stay in the shadows.

The second option was to duck into the woods behind him. It was a little further than the distance to the shed. Once there, he would need to fight his way through the thick underbrush without any light to guide the way, and it would be noisy. It would take longer, but Gunner decided that this was the best option.

He took two short gasps, counted to one, and ripped the tarp off his body. He sprinted as fast as his aching knee would allow and practically dove into the thicket. Sticks went flying as the exasperated man came to a halt. He gasped for air as he turned and looked behind him. Nothing had changed.

Gunner's thoughts began to percolate and evaporate just as quickly. He felt an extreme sense of urgency and decided it was time to regroup. Maybe he should.... But what if...? Then he could.... Not until.... What if...? The young man gritted his teeth and smacked the side of his head. *Focus!* he screamed inside his head. *What's the next task?*

The flustered man remembered the tree with the porthole. He knew he could at least grab the gear he'd brought with him. He wasn't sure if his other rifle was still in the shed. Gunner decided his best course of action at this moment was to gather his bag and hidden rifle. He could then decide what to do after that task was accomplished.

The young hunter tried to move as stealthily as he could, but it was proving to be quite difficult. Little black burs and pointy sticks kept poking and prodding his body as he made a half circle around Emmerson's property. Sometimes it felt like the underbrush was trying to pull him down to be swallowed into the ground. Nevertheless, Gunner traversed through the sea of dead foliage.

Every so often, he would pause and crouch down to try to calm his nerves and collect himself. His arms and hands felt hot and wet from all the scratches. It was too dark to tell if blood or sweat was causing the stinging discomfort. Gunner forced his mind to remain on the task of finding his bag and rifle. He was deep enough into the woods that he couldn't see the edge of the yard, which was a good thing considering all the noise the broken sticks and fallen leaves were making.

The moon was still hovering in the sky to the left of his current position, so the determined man was navigating in the correct direction. Gunner could barely make it out, but it was enough to guide him to where he needed to be. He couldn't help but notice the complete silence as he sat crouched near the ground. The eerie stillness left an ominous feeling, so he decided to keep moving.

After he maneuvered around a large stump, he glanced through the distant opening in the trees. The dingy light was still creeping along the wispy grass towards the front of the house. He couldn't see the shed, so he must have passed it. The young man looked down and noticed a subtle trail of misplaced branches and leaves. He followed the path deeper into the woods.

Sure enough, Gunner stumbled back upon the tree with the porthole. A slight sense of relief washed over him when he reached down and grabbed his gear. The relief instantly vanished when he realized he didn't have a plan now that this task was completed.

He sat down and leaned his head against the base of a tree. He looked up at the sky and noticed the stars were gleaming brightly, sprinkled across the black canvas. Gunner wished he could just float up into the sky and disappear among the stars. He imagined soaring through the air above the trees like a hawk, drifting at his own pace in whichever direction he chose. He could let the wind guide him until he felt like finding a suitable destination.

The thoughts of flying quickly dissolved as the memory of the young woman's face seeped into his mind. The young man's thoughts turned to being trapped in the shed with her, consumed by darkness. All of a sudden, he felt completely alone.

Gunner reached into his bag and grabbed his binoculars. He scanned the yard in front of the house. He spotted the broken truck and outline of the shed. It didn't look like anyone had gone in there yet. He then scanned the driveway. "Holy shit," he whispered to himself.

Officer Renard had driven her cruiser out there. That meant she must have been on duty, or was about to be. It also meant she probably had a dashcam in the vehicle, so Gunner sure as hell couldn't risk being seen going back to the shed to grab his rifle. If she had one, she would surely erase the footage unless she had a legitimate reason to pay Emmerson a visit. Gunner didn't want to risk it. This meant he didn't have much time because the officer wouldn't be able to stay at this location very long.

* * *

A thin blanket of white snow began to stick to the naked tree branches as it descended from the sky. Puffy flakes would accumulate on the ground in spotty patches. The grass had already begun to retreat deep into the soil in preparation for the cruel winter months.

The first snowfall of the year was always a beautiful melancholy. Each unique flake would silently fall with grace and leave a white glimmer wherever it landed. This was the purest it would be all season before it would be cast to the ground and blended with earthly elements in between deep freezes and occasional thaws. It also meant the ground would be hidden for the next three to four months, and a lingering icy chill would soon be an unwanted guest.

Jan continued his trek, his .22 caliber rifle slung over his shoulder. The snow was making it difficult to track the light pawprints in the dirt. The ground wasn't frozen, but it was becoming calloused. The dirt was softer here because a small pond sat nearby.

A friend of Fredrick's had complained that his

hens were starting to disappear. A bold intruder had been furtive while stalking its prey and remained elusive so far. The friend had a pretty good idea of what the culprit was but decided to consult Frederick and Jan nonetheless. The two investigated the crime scene and concluded that a fox had been sneaking around the area in search of an easy dinner. Now that the animal had a taste for an abundant food source, it would continue to be a nuisance.

Jan had taken it upon himself to track the animal alone. This wasn't the first time someone had asked for their help in protecting livestock, but the adolescent always felt like he was just tagging along on his father's hunts. He was approaching his teenage years and wanted to prove that he could take care of the situation on his own. Frederick had objected at first, but after numerous protests from his son, he saw how much it really meant to him.

The fox den was probably within a mile or two of the hen house, considering the weather was getting colder. Foxes didn't typically hibernate but kept to themselves during late fall. They also made sure they had a supply of food nearby.

As Jan pressed on, he started to lose track of the pawprints. The owner had said that one of his hens had been taken the night before, so the tracks were fresh. The problem was that foxes were lightweight and didn't leave a very big impression. Now that the ground was getting harder and the light snow had begun to fall, it was becoming nearly impossible to hunt the sly creature.

Jan felt the frustration start to boil under his skin. He was starting to wander further and further from the soft dirt near the pond. He was losing the trail and becoming increasingly agitated at the prospect of returning empty-handed. Even though his father would tell him it was okay and that it was his first solo fox hunt, the young hunter didn't want to feel like a disappointment. He desperately wanted to return with pelt in hand, feeling like the hero.

The determined hunter circled back to where the trail had started to go cold. The den had to be in close proximity, given the distance between the food and water supplies. He closed his eyes and made a mental picture of the area. The pond was to his left, the henhouse about a mile directly behind him, and a small clearing directly in front of him. The snow-capped trees lined a gently sloping hill to his right. Jan opened his eyes and stared at the ground as if trying to see an X-ray of tiny pawprints hidden underneath the surface. It was no use guessing which way the fox had gone.

He decided his best option would be to try to lure the animal to him. His instincts were dragging him toward the small clearing in the forest directly in front of him. The young hunter could almost feel the animal's presence nearby, kind of like a sixth sense. Hopefully, it hadn't caught his scent yet. They could spend days hiding out in their dens this time of year.

Jan forged ahead and made his way to the opening between the trees. He waited underneath the shelter of a heavy pine tree branch. The young hunter searched the clearing for a place to conceal his body. The space was mostly open except for a few rogue pine trees and a large rock near the center. The rock would have to suffice since it was near the center of the clearing and created the best vantage point.

The tenacious young hunter made his way toward the rock. He twisted off a few low-lying pine branches along the way to cover his legs as he propped himself against the cold hard surface. The pine fragrance overwhelmed his nose, but it was somewhat refreshing.

The snowflakes started to feel heavier now that nothing was keeping them from dropping to the ground. Jan brushed the snow off his glove before reaching into his pocket and pulling out a whistle. He rubbed it between his gloves, pressed the cold device to his lips, and blew. The sound that came from the whistle was somewhat startling because it was designed to mimic an injured rabbit.

Jan mustered three powerful, loud shrieks of the whistle. The sound resonated through the clearing and drifted into the forest. If the fox was nearby, it would hear the harrowing noise. The hunter squinted and looked for movement in between the fluttering snowflakes. The silence made it easier to concentrate. He sat motionless for a few minutes, waiting to see if anything stirred.

Jan didn't blink once as he waited patiently. He felt a heightened sense of his surroundings, and his mind was calm and calculating as he focused on his task. There was nothing stirring yet, so he put the whistle back to his lips and made a slower, low pitched sound. This was to simulate a weakened rabbit. The young hunter waited again to see if the fox would come to investigate.

Hopefully, the keen creature would be curious enough to at least check on an easy meal, even though it had just stolen a hen the night before. The snow was starting to accumulate, so it would be extremely difficult to try to pick up its trail again. The longer Jan waited, the lower his heart sank at the possibility of returning with his tail between his legs. He waited about ten minutes and decided to blow a long, low whistle.

Jan waited, still motionless and determined to wait for the fox. His eyes thoroughly swept every inch between the green and white edges of the forest. Every snowflake that graced him might as well have been a lead ball pelting his skin. Time was running out, and his frustration would soon get the best of him.

Then out of the corner of his left eye, Jan caught a blur of brown movement that disappeared behind a large pine tree. A mix of elation and adrenaline soared through his body. The young hunter remained calm and gave a soft low pitched whistle. Seconds dragged on like years as he patiently waited. He positioned his gun around the side of the rock and waited.

Just before the young hunter's heart burst out his chest, the curious face reemerged in the clearing. Jan took careful aim and forcefully squeezed the trigger. The shot struck the animal in the chest and dropped it instantly. The young hunter sat by the rock for a few minutes to bask in the feat he had just accomplished.

* * *

Gunner's hands were tightly wrapped around the steering wheel of his SUV. The seatbelt was strapped as firmly as possible across his midsection. The vehicle sat idling alone on the deserted highway beneath the cloudless black sky.

The desperate man looked down at the odometer and watched the red needle spike a few times after revving the engine. He gradually eased the idle up to thirty mph. Once he was satisfied he was applying the correct pressure, he took his foot off the gas paddle and stared through his windshield into the darkness.

It was beautiful, really, the way the trees stood defiantly along the side of the road that was thrown in their path. Their leaves were tossed on the pavement in protest. The cultivated field that had been so full of life until very recently was mending its wounds to prepare to sow seeds again next season. The dirt was still lying in discombobulated clumps, waiting to settle and return to its resting place for the winter.

Gunner took in his surroundings one last time. He closed his eyes and painted a picture of what he had just seen in his mind. He then lowered his head and clenched his teeth. "Here we go," he muttered to himself. His foot slammed on the gas pedal, and he drove straight toward his target. He barely had time to glance at the odometer to see he was going faster than thirty mph. The vehicle drifted off the highway, and tires rattled when they hit the ditch. The last image he saw was the trunk of a massive tree crushing the hood of his SUV.

The impact jolted the young man's entire body. A metallic taste filled the inside of his mouth. He must have bit the inside of his cheek after the impact. Everything looked a bit blurry too. Gunner reached for the seatbelt, but a sharp pain shot through his lower back.

He decided to wait a few minutes and let his body adjust from the collision. He sat with his head pressed back against the headrest and closed his eyes. The young man waited patiently for a few minutes and did a mental scan of his body to see how he was feeling. Suddenly a strange man's voice startled him back to the present moment.

"Hi, this is Thomas with On Point, and I just got a notification that your vehicle has been in an accident. I want to make sure everyone is all right. Can you hear me?"

Gunner responded, "Yeah, I'm okay, just a little sore. A deer jumped in front of me, and I ran off the road."

Thomas replied, "Okay, I am trying to send your location to the authorities, but the impact must have disrupted your GPS. Do you know your location? It is just a necessary precaution."

Gunner remembered the green mile marker sign near the side of the road before he drove into the tree. "Yeah, I can see the 21-mile marker on Highway 36."

"Perfect. And am I speaking with Mr. Jan Sorenson?" Thomas asked.

"That is correct," Gunner replied. It was kind of weird responding to a disembodied voice coming from his car speakers.

"Okay, Mr. Sorenson. It looks like a cruiser is in the vicinity and will be dispatched shortly. Just hang tight."

"Thanks," Gunner simply replied.

He pulled out both of his phones. Before crashing into the tree, he had put the SIM card back into his main phone and texted himself the gruesome picture. Gunner forced himself to make sure the picture had downloaded and saved on his main phone. He then opened his browser and scrolled down the page to the email link that was highlighted in blue. He clicked on it, and a "compose email" message flooded his screen.

"I hope this works," the frenzied man whispered to himself. He attached the photo to the email message and laid the phone on the empty seat next to him. He put his burner phone back into his pocket and reached down again to unlock his seatbelt. The sharp pain was still there but not quite as intense.

Gunner opened his car door and spit a crimson stain onto the grass. The hood of his SUV was transformed into an accordion. The tree was mostly intact, except for some bark that had been shredded as a result of the collision with steel.

The young man had never been in a car accident before. He tried to remember the events leading up to the crash, but everything happened so fast. It felt like one minute he was testing the gas pedal, and the next minute he was keeled over on the ground. There was a bit of shock even if his intentions were deliberate. He tried to imagine what it would have been like if a deer really had jumped in front of him and caused his SUV to veer off the road.

The unnerved man opened the side door of the SUV and pulled out his black bag. He unzipped it and slid it underneath the vehicle behind the front tire. He tried to bend down and place some tall weeds around it, but the redundant pain exploded down his side. He grunted in anger more than anything. The frustrated man decided it would have to do as he gingerly sat down in the cool soft grass.

Just then, a flicker of blue light caught his eye from the reflection in his rearview mirror. It was quickly getting brighter with each flash. Gunner stood as fast as his aching body would allow. He crawled over the driver's seat and grabbed his phone. Instinct took over as he firmly pressed the Send button without a trace of hesitation. The swoosh sound that came after the message was sent might as well have been a drill bit burrowing into his ear drums. There was no turning back now.

The anxious man threw his phone into his pocket and crawled out of the vehicle to lie in the grass by the front tire. He waited for the cruiser to approach. The grass was still settling around him when the cruiser finally came to a stop. Shades of red and blue were bouncing off the trees. The car door slammed, and tentative footsteps approached.

Gunner let out a low moan that was mostly buried in the grass.

"Mr. Sorensen? Can you hear me?" Officer Renard called.

Gunner waited a few seconds before gently lifting his head and replying, "What happened?"

Renard retorted, "You were in a car accident. Just lie still. I'll call for an ambulance."

Gunner ignored her request and began to sit up. He rubbed his head and the back of his neck. He closed his eyes almost all the way, but he could still see the outline of Officer Renard's body from his peripheral. She was more concerned with the inside of the SUV.

"Fuckin deer jumped in front of me," Gunner mumbled. The officer reached for her flashlight and began spraying narrow beams through the back window. Every now and then, she would shine the light toward the front of the vehicle as if she were investigating the damage. As her focus grazed toward the rear bumper, Gunner slid his hand through the grass and rested it on the black bag.

"You're lucky your vehicle didn't flip," the officer stated flatly. She was now behind the vehicle staring intently through the rear window. Something must have caught her attention. She casually tried to lift the handle on the door, but it wouldn't budge. The beam of light didn't waver until she noticed the open car door next to Gunner. Renard made a few lackluster sweeps of the flashlight and then started walking toward the front of the SUV.

"I'm lucky you were in the area," Gunner groaned. He was now sitting in front of the open door with his hands behind his back. "Who knows how long it would have taken someone to get here from town?"

Renard narrowed her eyes and hesitated before responding, "I just happened to be on patrol at the right time and place." Her eyes briefly glanced off into the distance to her left. She was still gripping the flashlight in one hand, and the other found its way to her belt. "So, what were you doing out this way?" she asked accusingly.

Gunner lowered his head and started to take slow wheezy breaths. His hands were now resting inside of the hidden black bag. "I was on my way to one of the bonfire parties," he labored through his raspy breathing.

Renard shifted her weight between restless feet, her eyes prodding Gunner's crumpled body. "I didn't see too many lights from the highway all the way out here," she said. Her hand slunk to the leather case on the side of her hip.

The slumped over man gave a deep cough and spit into the grass next to his leg. His finger found its way to the safety lock inside the black bag during the process. He groaned and let out a weak sigh. "How's that ambulance coming?" he asked.

The officer stood silently for a moment, her eyes shifting slightly to the rear window of the SUV. Her face looked as though she were calculating a very difficult math equation. She lowered the flashlight in a slow and deliberate motion. The concentrated beam burned the grass next to her onyx boots. Her index finger fluttered at the leather strap on her side. Her face sunk like a stone to the bottom of a lake, drowning in remorse. Before she could whisper an apologetic excuse, her walkie broke the suffocating silence.

"All units! All units! Possible 10-54. Please respond!"

Officer Renard looked at her walkie as if it were sending Morse code. The brief distraction was all that Gunner needed to swing the gun from behind his back and aim it at Ms. Renard. It took a second for her to register what had just happened.

Gunner's head was throbbing, but his finger was cold and steady. "Don't try what I think you're gonna try," he said in a clear, stern voice. "This doesn't have to get messy. You might have a way out of this."

Renard almost looked impressed. Her hand was still attached to the leather strap on her hip. "I knew I shouldn't have let you out of my sight," she said. "No one will believe anything you say, and I'm still closest to the scene. You should have just minded your own fucking business."

Gunner sat unflinching. "It's kinda hard when people are stalking me and framing me for murder," he replied.

Renard scoffed and looked defiantly down the barrel of the gun pointed at her face. "I was dragged into this. You didn't even know the girl, but you had to go poking around in places you don't belong. You just so happened to be out in the woods doing God knows what in the middle of the fucking night. I'm not going to let some low-life alcoholics take me down because they can't keep their shit together."

Gunner sat motionless, letting Renard's words wriggle inside his head. She probably wasn't going to shoot him. There was no way she would be able to unstrap her pistol and get a shot off before he could, even if she was Annie Oakley. And she was absolutely right. She was the closest to the house and could easily take care of Emerson. Then it would be his word against hers. He still wasn't even completely sure what was in the back of his SUV that kept stealing her attention.

"I was afraid it would come to this," Gunner said. He squeezed the trigger, and the familiar ringing invaded his eardrums.

* * *

Jamie stepped out of the bathroom, and her skin was immediately greeted by the cold air of her bedroom. A warm mist swirled above her head as she tightened the white towel around her damp hair. She thought the much-needed shower would have calmed her nerves, but she still felt like she was walking on pins and needles.

The young woman tightened her robe as she walked over to her closet and clicked on the light. She started rummaging through her hanging shirts, each one getting angrily slung across the rack the more she realized she had prematurely overturned her wardrobe to winter sweaters and thermal shirts. That meant most of her summer shirts and tank tops were either buried in the back of the closet or sitting at the bottom of her dresser drawers.

She turned around and stared at the contents of the open suitcase sprawled across the bed. So far, she had been able to find her travel-sized deodorant, toothpaste, and mouthwash, but nothing else. She had barely remembered where the gray suitcase had been stored, let alone her travel necessities. If anything, it would give her an impromptu excuse to fill a red cart at Target in the near future.

Jamie grabbed her phone from the nightstand and scrolled to the top of the webpage. The yellow "complete your order" box taunted, almost dared her to give it a little tap with her finger. She felt like if she breathed hard enough, the phone would be able to sense her hesitation and know to complete the order for her. Jan would be pissed when he found the credit card statement, but that was the least of her worries right now.

Before she could tap the screen, Jamie remembered the money belt she liked to use when she traveled. It was small enough to fit around her waist underneath her clothes, but it could safely store all her credit cards, photo ID, and a small bundle of cash. She hated having a TSA agent rummage through her personal items in her purse at the security line, so it was more convenient to toss the empty purse with her luggage. That way, she wouldn't have to worry about losing it or having it stolen.

The money belt, along with their passports, was usually stored in Jan's top dresser drawer. She never was one to rummage through his personal things or spy on his text messages and emails, but she was pretty sure she knew exactly where it was hiding. The thought of trying to ask him to find it if and when he came home tonight made her skin crawl, so she decided to make an exception and stealthily search for the belt.

His drawer creaked as Jamie slowly pried it open, sending a shudder down her spine. Had it really come to this? That one gentle tug of the handle felt like a marriage betrayal that could never be undone, but there was no turning back now. She decided to open it all the way.

She guiltily rummaged through his socks and plain white T-shirts as her fingers searched for the money belt. The deeper her fingers pried, the more random junk they seemed to graze. She pulled out some expired drivers licenses, a rusted Swiss army knife, and some kind of furry orangish tail that looked like it was once attached to a keychain.

The longer the drawer hung open, the more Jamie's anxiety began to asphyxiate her. She just wanted to find the belt and slam the drawer closed before she made a complete mess of everything. Just as she was about to slam the drawer shut in a fit of panic, her fingers grazed an elastic strap toward the back of the drawer.

The frazzled young woman ripped the belt from the back of the drawer, but it got caught on something and flipped a few things onto the bedroom floor. She frantically threw the belt into the open suitcase and bent down to pick up what was flung on the floor. A pair of black socks was lying next to a passport and what looked like a poker chip or something. Jamie picked everything up and placed them carefully back in the drawer, but she curiously pulled the chip out for a closer examination.

It was heavier than it looked. She turned it over in her fingers and read the front. There was a golden triangle with three words written along each side: unity, service, and recovery. The words "Three Months" were inscribed in the middle of the triangle.

Jamie thought her husband had tossed anything associated with AA in the trash. She couldn't remember the last time he talked about going to a meeting. The word cult was used on more than one occasion when he actually talked about it, which was only a handful of times. Jamie had offered to go with him for support in the early stages of his recovery, but he was always quick to dismiss the idea. He constantly went about things in his own way, which was usually by himself.

Jamie let those feelings of frustration and powerlessness course through her before gently setting the chip on top of Jan's dresser. She turned back toward the mostly unoccupied suitcase and stared for a few minutes. She realized she didn't have the energy to go searching for everything she needed tonight.

The exhausted woman unwrapped the white towel from her head and heedlessly tossed it on the tiled bathroom floor. All she wanted to do was slide into bed and let the events of the day fade into tomorrow. She threw the money belt in the suitcase before flipping it shut and sliding it underneath the bed like a misbehaving kid hiding the evidence of a guilty deed. Even if Jan came tonight, he would more than likely sleep it off on the couch, but Jamie didn't want to risk a fight. She closed the bedroom door, flicked off the light, and fell into a deep sleep as soon as her damp hair hit the soft pillow.

CHAPTER TEN

Steam was rising from the white Styrofoam cup of stale sludge that was placed in front of Gunner. He sat nervously in an uncomfortable chair, debating if he should try to sip it with his free hand. The metal cuff on his right hand was starting to chafe his wrist. The aroma of cheap coffee was nauseating. Maybe it was poison. The only thing missing was some narcissistic asshole telling grandiose stories of his borderline former self. The difference was that at those gatherings, Gunner could choose to opt out of sharing his story without having to retain a lawyer.

The door swiftly opened, and Officer Stansby walked in, his face drooping and his eyes almost sunken behind puffy black lumps. His mustache was still neatly trimmed, and his shirt was tightly tucked in, though. He didn't waste any time after he took a seat across from Gunner and asked, "So how is it, again, that your rifle ended up in the same shed where that poor girl was found?"

Gunner let out an extra-long raspy sigh. He began to wonder if it was the lack of sleep, dim fluorescent lighting, or the repeated questions that were causing the stabbing pain in his forehead. Suddenly the sludge didn't seem like such a bad idea. Did cyanide leave a bitter aftertaste?

"Like I told you before, I was talking to my wife and her little sidekick at the bonfire party off of Sandborne Drive, and when I went back to my SUV, I noticed someone was walking in the other direction with something large. I noticed my cab light was on and the fact that my rifle was missing."

Stansby wrote something on his notepad. It couldn't have been Gunner's statement because they had a few of those already. The sternness never left the officer's face as he paged through some documents. Maybe he was going to line the statements up and try to play Connect Four with the words.

He paused for a minute and said, "Yeah, we talked to Jamie, Allison, and a few other people, and they all claimed to remember you being there briefly around eight. But there is quite a gap in time between then when you say you saw someone with your rifle and when your vehicle was reported in an accident with On Point at roughly ten-forty-five."

There were certainly holes in the raft, but Gunner knew how to patch them well enough to stay afloat, at least until it made it back to dry land. He shifted around in the metal chair as if it were covered in barbed wire. Didn't they have to give him a mandatory break to stretch his legs every so often?

"Yeah. I wanted to know what I was getting myself into before just chasing after someone that had stolen my rifle. I'd say it was a pretty smart move on my part, all things considered," Gunner replied. "I followed them back to that shitty excuse for a hideout and staked it out for a while."

Stansby dropped the documents and let his pen roll off the end of the table. He stared at Gunner for an antagonizing minute. The poor guy was trying his hardest to make sense of everything that had just happened within the last few days. It was like looking at a statue that had been beaten down by harsh weather, its foundation beginning to crack.

He bellowed, "And the GPS in your SUV somehow got disabled, and your phone went dead conveniently within that timeframe? You just fell off the face of the earth, went all incognito, and happened to stumble upon this atrocity?"

The foundation was starting to crumble. Wasn't Gunner supposed to be the one to unravel first? The young man thought about asking to speak to a lawyer, but he didn't want to seem guilty. He was already in custody, willingly, and they had him cuffed to a chair. It was like when you got sent to the principal's office, and he or she threw a stack of formal documents in front of you and threatened expulsion if you didn't cooperate. The police hadn't officially charged him with anything yet, so Gunner decided he wanted to keep playing.

"I told you, I can't explain how that happened. It must have been a strange coincidence."

This probably infuriated Stansby, but he wouldn't give Gunner the satisfaction of showing it. Instead, he picked up his pen and recomposed himself. He sifted through the stack of papers and pulled out a photo. He slid it over to Gunner and solemnly said, "And how did you know to send this picture to the chief of police's email address and that we would know what to do? Most people would have just dialed 911."

Gunner glanced at the gruesome photo but had to look away. Stansby was studying his reaction, probably trying to throw him off his game. The young man flipped the photo over and responded, "I knew photos taken with a cell phone are coded with GPS coordinates. I knew I was in danger, so I gambled and sent the photo, trusting someone would know how to pull that information. I'm glad you guys were able to respond so quickly."

Stansby scoffed and gave an amused grunt. He clasped his big hands together and rested them underneath his chin. Gunner couldn't tell if the officer was actually impressed or just being facetious.

"And you just so happened to get your phone charged up minutes before getting into a car accident, but sent the email after the wreck and right before shooting Renard in the arm. Another amazingly lucky coincidence?"

Gunner decided to tread lightly. Even if Renard had broken the law and put Gunner's life at risk, she still wore the same badge and uniform as Stansby. Plus, they had been over the series of events a few times already. Stansby must have had something else besides the cell phone photo up his sleeve.

"I wanted to be sure I wasn't being followed. I was planning on going straight to the station, but the deer jumped in front of me like I told you before. Renard was the first officer on scene, and she didn't seem too concerned about calling an ambulance. She even pulled her gun on me." The young man half-expected the music to cut him off before he was done with his Academy Award speech.

Stansby half-heartedly glanced at his documents.

"Yeah, we got the whole conversation between you and Renard recorded and in evidence, courtesy of On Point. Again, since both of you were conveniently out of view of her cruiser dashcam, we just have the tape to go on as evidence."

The officer hadn't let that detail slip until now. It seemed like a bold move to present the evidence against the person in custody. Gunner didn't respond. He just waited for Stansby to make the next move. Maybe he would turn the cameras off and have a few officers step in to "reprimand an unruly suspect." They would take turns fucking up a cop shooter...a cop shooter who was handcuffed to a steel chair. But at least he wasn't a cop killer. That had to count for something.

Stansby broke the weary man's train of thought by saying, "We could charge you with enough stuff to make your life miserable for the foreseeable future, but for some reason, the prosecutors want nothing to do with you. They got that degenerate drunk, Emmerson, to turn on Renard and confess to the whole thing. She is being implicated as an accomplice who wanted to frame you in order to prove herself as an up-and-coming deputy. In fact, they're willing to look past the shooting if you agree to testify in court. Apparently, a shoulder graze is admissible given this type of circumstantial self-defense."

Gunner waited for the officer to finally crack a smile or to give a jovial wink toward the camera in the corner of the ceiling. The man's face remained a marble facade, the last piece to stay intact. Why wasn't the prosecution team explaining this? As if reading Gunner's mind, the officer spoke again.

"This is a high-profile crime for these parts. The girl, Clara Ellsbury, was a sweet middle-class kid who had just graduated college. There is a lot of pressure to get a conviction and close this case. The media and her family want justice, and I don't blame them."

The young man wondered when Stansby was going to step off his soapbox. Did he want a medal for following the billowing smoke and finding the raging fire? Maybe he would get a key to the city.

Stansby continued. "I did a little digging these past few days. The coroner put the time of death at around 5:00 a.m. She had an early shift at the hospital, so she was probably out for a jog before work. Your cell phone was pinged at the tower near Evansville, about thirty miles from the nearest tower to your house and the closest tower to the scene of the crime. Now, why the fuck would your cell phone be in range of that tower at that specific time?"

Gunner's heart stopped. The metal cuff seared his skin. He could almost smell his skin grafting to the metal. Maybe now would be a good time to lawyer up.

Before he could say anything, Stansby replied, "I know you're not telling me everything. And my hands are tied in this clusterfuck of a case. But I know goddamn well you're not the stupid, degenerate badass you act like. In fact, I'm pretty sure the apple didn't fall too far from the tree, but it probably rolled down the hill when the tree was cut down. So here is what's going to happen. Since I've been advised to not pursue you any longer, you're going to walk out of here today. But you're not going to be the hero. If and when I find anything to charge you with, whether it's related to this case or not, I'm going to drop the hammer on you. So, choose your actions carefully from here on out."

Stansby didn't even wait for a response. He just tossed Gunner the key and walked out of the room. The door was left open, the clink of the key still echoing in the room.

* * *

Jan was pacing between a large ash tree and the back of the old green pick-up truck. It was parked just off a lightly traveled gravel road. Fredrick refused to let the rusted clunker retire because it was still somewhat reliable. The bed was big enough to haul their supplies and anything they might be fortunate enough to bring back from their excursions. If it got them from point A to point B, there was no sense in investing in another vehicle just yet.

Fredrick was pulling his supplies out of his bag and repacking them after crossing them off his mental checklist. He always did this before they left the house and before they set out on foot. It usually drove Jan nuts, and today was no exception. The youthful adolescent would usually focus his energy on tightening his bowstring tension or making sure the tips of his arrows could practically pierce rocks, but his arrows were laying in an erratic mess from the middle of the bed to the tailgate of the truck. His bow was dangling from his elbow, skipping off the ground every few steps.

The whole ride out here had been used to plead a case to Fredrick to start calling him by his middle name. "Tommy, Ryan, and some other boys from class keep calling me Janet and won't pick me to be on their teams

at recess. They say they don't want a girl on their team."
Fredrick had refused to entertain the notion and dismissed
the pleads with audible sighs between sips of his coffee.

When he was sure everything they needed was
accounted for, he had Jan pick up his arrows, arrange them
in neat rows, and carefully file them in his quiver. The
two of them then set out on foot into the heavily wooded
forest. A purple hue of dawn left a ring around the eastern
horizon. As they were walking toward the next location of
their tree stand, Jan kept getting his quiver strap caught
on branches and dropping his arrows. The adolescent
was grunting louder and throwing his arrows back into
the quiver harder each time this happened. It got to the
point that Fredrick had to remind him that he still wanted
the deer to be in the same zip code by the time they were
settled in the tree stand.

The summer had been rough on Jan. He had spent
a lot of time watching reruns of black and white television
shows at his grandmother's house. Her pesky arthritis
kept her seated in her knitting chair most days, and her
only deck of cards had yellow frayed edges with pictures
of Elvis on them. It was hard to find a decent babysitter
that was willing to work for free. It was harder to convince
Jan that he wasn't mature enough to take care of himself
while he was away from school.

After a few more stumbles with the quiver, the
two finally arrived at an adequate cluster of bulky trees to
assemble their seasoned perches. Frederick unzipped his
bag and pulled out his collapsible ladder. The contraption
was a unique design of his own that came in handy when
he didn't want to haul a traditional ladder on a long trek

through the woods, especially one that didn't fit into his bag. As he unfolded it and stacked it against the next base for his foreseeable vantage point, Jan took a pointed arrow and began stabbing leaves from the ground while gently humming. The point was so sharp that the brittle leaves stayed unscathed as they accumulated up the shaft. Before his arrow became a skewer for frying leaves over a fire, Frederick asked for help setting up his platform.

Jan slapped the flakes off his arrow, reached down to grab the straps, and tossed them up to his father. The first one missed and fell to the other side of the tree. Jan grunted and kicked his boot against the base of the tree. The second toss hit Frederick on the leg, but he was able to catch it with his foot. He was able to secure the straps around the robust tree trunk by himself before climbing down to assemble the platform.

The platform was basically just a plank that would jut out from the base of the tree about ten to fifteen feet above the ground. The straps were the only thing that would support the weight of the platform, person, and usually a chair. That is why Frederick always double-checked his own work and made sure everything was secured properly. Once he had his perch and chair assembled to his liking, he asked his son if he was ready to assemble his. When there was no answer, he begrudgingly called Jan to come back to assemble his own stand.

The boy had wandered a good thirty yards from the vantage point and was either building an enormous slingshot or testing the flexibility of a few fallen branches. The cracking and splitting pops of dried wood was starting to seep into the father's ears and travel through his body, only to settle right beneath his skin. As Jan moseyed his way back, Frederick climbed up to his own perch and readied himself to lie in wait.

The elder Sorenson took a seat in his chair and admired the streaks of morning sun filtering through the tops of the trees. His breath would swirl like mist every time he exhaled, eventually drifting up and evaporating into what was left of the night. The only thing that could have made the fresh morning even more perfect would have been a fire, but that would surely scare away all the deer. A little silence from his son wouldn't hurt either.

Jan spent the next twenty minutes getting increasingly frustrated trying to assemble his own stand. He had done it dozens of times before, but his mind and body were on two different pages this morning. Every time he would groan loud enough for his father to hear, Jan would look up at Frederick long enough to notice that he hadn't moved once since climbing into his own stand. The boy refused to ask for help.

Frederick listened to the exasperation as long as he could before finally crawling down from his perch. If his son wasn't careful, he would neglect properly strapping the platform and risk injuring himself. Tears had welled in the boy's eyes by now, and the straps were on the verge of getting twisted. Together they silently finished assembling the stand and got ready to lure their prey.

After a few minutes of inactivity, Jan started shifting in the stand and fidgeting with his arrows. They were dangerously close to just calling the morning a wash, packing it up, and going home with nothing to show for their efforts. Frederick gently pulled the boy close to him and whispered, "Get your arrow ready."

A light went on inside the boy's eyes, and he regained a bit of focus. He looked around beneath them and put his arrow against the bow string.

"What do we do when we tighten the string?" the father asked.

Jan was a bit confused, but he drew some tension on the string and breathed in deep. The breath was held for about four seconds and then slowly and silently released through his mouth. He scanned the area and gently released the tension a bit on the string. He didn't see anything below, but he continued to breathe as if he was about to release a kill shot. This went on for a few minutes before he heard a whisper. "Just making sure you're ready."

Jan's shoulders relaxed, and he took a seat in his chair. Frederick told him that he would consider using his middle name if he recited the steps they would take to lure the deer to them. After every whispered answer, the father would simply whisper back, "And the next task?"... "And the next task?"... "Then what?"...

Each exchange between the two got quieter and softer until they basically had to read each other's lips. They resorted to communicating in hand signals for the rest of the morning. After prolonged inactivity, Frederick helped his son practice the breathing exercises. Every so often, he would pretend to snore and get a stifled chuckle from the boy. They didn't bring home a prize that day, but Jan sat perfectly still with a reticent poise in his own stand from early morning until he disassembled the perch himself.

* * *

A cupboard slammed in the bare kitchen as Gunner took the lone frying pan and placed it on the stove. He flipped on the gas and put his hand next to the blue flame. The little bit of heat was welcoming now that a layer of white dust continually brushed against the windows. He had enough wood sitting in the garage to keep the fire in the main room going, but it was heating an empty couch on the other side of the house.

The young man glanced at his phone and checked the weather in Fresno, California: seventy-one degrees and sunny. He smiled as he began unwrapping a white blood-stained package of meat. As he waited for the pan to heat up, Gunner rinsed his hands and dried them on a paper towel. When he went to toss the towel away, he decided to grab the formal letter that had been tossed on the counter and rip it open.

Dear Mr. Sorenson,
We thank you for your cooperation with our office and for your service as a witness. We appreciate the sacrifice of your time that being a witness requires.

Gunner crumpled up the letter after reading the gist of it. He was just glad the shitstorm was over. He could go three lifetimes without ever talking to a lawyer again. The only good thing that came from being on a first name basis with the prosecution was learning that cell phone evidence, especially reception from a specific tower during a precise timeframe, was unreliable and won't hold up in court. Even so, he decided it wouldn't be such a bad idea to keep a low profile, given the circumstances.

The young man grabbed a curved filet knife and began cutting the meat into thin strips. The meat was a little tough, but the knife carved through it with relative ease. Blood dripped down the handle of the knife as it tore through, making it hard for Gunner to keep a decent grip. He decided the strips were thin enough, so he walked over to the sink to wash his hands.

Before he could turn the faucet on, his phone gave a startling rattle and played an obnoxious jingle from the counter. He glanced at the screen and noticed a familiar area code. Normally he didn't answer numbers that weren't saved as contacts, but he hastily washed his hands, pushed the green button, and simply mumbled, "Hello?"

The female voice on the other end replied, "Hey, Mr. Sorenson. Sorry to call you from my cell phone, but I just wanted to call and tell you we received an offer on your house."

The house hadn't even been on the market very long, so this caught Gunner by surprise. "Wow, already? How much did they offer?"

"Well, they came in at about ten thousand under the list price, but that was to be expected."

The young man held the phone to his ear with his shoulder as he threw the meat on the sizzling frying pan. "Should I counter with another price?" He grabbed a partially burned spatula and arranged the meat into neat rows.

"Well, it is a good location with a decent-sized lot. It hasn't been on the market very long, so you might get more interest if you stay at the list price for now. Unless, of course, you want to move right now."

She was good. Gunner wanted nothing to do with the negotiation process. It was a stupid game that some people loved to play. His realtor was one of them.

"Well, if you think I should hold out a little longer, I can wait for now." He took the spatula and flipped the meat. The young man opened a bag of tortillas and placed three of them on a plate.

"Trust me, I've been doing this for a while, and I'm quite certain we can get a bidding war started."

Gunner opened the fridge and grabbed some lime and homemade salsa. "Okay, I'll trust you. Tell them the price is firm, and we'll wait a little longer." He placed the items on the table and grabbed the last of the clean silverware from the drawer.

"Excellent! I know it's tempting to jump on the first offer, but you won't be disappointed. Thank you for trusting me, Gunnar."

He placed the silverware on the table and walked back over to the frying pan. The meat was nicely crisp all the way through, so he turned off the stove. "Not a problem. And you can call me Jan."

There was a chuckle on the other end before she replied, "Sounds good. Have a good evening, Jan."

The young man hung up the phone and placed the meat in the tortillas. He took his phone and texted *Got an offer. It's a lil low, so gonna hold out a bit.* He then took the plate and walked over to the table. He doused the meat with lime juice and poured the chunky salsa onto the tortillas.

Jan took a minute to admire the meal he had

prepared. It had been a long time coming, and he wanted to relish this moment. As he sat and looked out the window, he noticed the familiar headlights of a car that seemed to be patrolling his street on a frequent basis lately. It just reinforced the decision to put the house on the market; start fresh somewhere new.

The phone vibrated and gave a minor bleep. He clicked on the message on the screen and saw a yellow smiley face emoji. The phone bleeped again, and the message read *Mom sends her luv*.

Jan put the phone down and grabbed his fork. He carefully cut a piece of tortilla and put it in his mouth. The bitterness of the meat could still be detected underneath the sour lime and spicy salsa. The meat was tough to chew, but it was the best meal the young man had eaten in a long time.

I'm Ash Nightengale, author of Howling at the Harvest Moon. Ever since I learned to read, I haven't been able to put down a book. I love reading other peoples' stories, but also creating my own. When I'm not formulating ideas for my next thriller novel or suspenseful short story, I enjoy playing fetch and trying to walk our lovable rescued goons: Piper - an energetic Greyhound/German Shepard mix and Romeo - a lover boy Jack Russel Terrier/Shih Tzu mix. They keep life interesting for my wife and me. We live in Minneapolis and enjoy spending time near some of the beautiful ten thousand lakes.

For more doggo and book content, follow my Instagram Account: @ash.nightengale

www.ingramcontent.com/pod-product-compliance
Lightning Source LLC
Chambersburg PA
CBHW020133180626
46810CB00004B/1527